Myth Blessed

Katie Dunn

Cover design by Phoenix Designs

ISBN-13: 9781699214985

Facebook.com/AuthorKatieDunn

Kdunnauthor.com

Titles by Katie Dunn

Ancient Elements

Pirates from Under

Myth Blessed

Table of Contents

Chapter 1

The Day I Almost Drowned

"Put your hand in the fire," the crazy lady said excitedly.

I stared, mouth agape, at the woman in the tropical shirt and sandy brown hair, sitting by the hotel fireplace. I looked around to see if anyone else heard the insane suggestion, but it was just us.

"I am not putting my hand in the fire!" I shouted.

My mother, aka crazy lady, pouted. "But how will we find out if you are blessed by a fire myth?"

I snorted in disbelief and scooted away from the fire. I was tired of reminding my parents that my myth blessed test results were negative. If I was myth blessed, I would have been identified by now, so it was pointless to keep testing me.

I leaned my head back and closed my eyes to wait for my dad. I just wanted to relax and enjoy my summer break in Hawaii. We had only arrived a few hours ago, and all we had done so far was check in and put on our stupid tourist shirts.

"One little touch of the flames would not hurt you," my mother persisted.

Sighing heavily, I stood and walked out of the hotel. Our hotel was right next to the beach, so I decided to run along the sand to get as far away as I could for a while. I needed a few minutes away from my mother and figured I could be back in time for our first tour. I really hoped she would put aside the myth blessed stuff for the rest of the trip, otherwise it would be a sucky vacation.

I used to hope for amazing abilities to manifest and sometimes I would daydream about which mythological creature blessed me. Then I turned thirteen, then fourteen. By fifteen, I had given up hope since abilities often manifested by thirteen. My parents constantly talked about it and still hoped I would show signs, but I was done dreaming about the impossible. By seventeen, I got orders to take the myth blessed test as required by law, and it came back negative. If that was not the final nail in the proverbial coffin for myth blessed hopes, I did not know what was.

I fell into a rhythm and soon thoughts of my mother and the negative results of my exam drifted away. I focused on my breathing and the sound of the waves, letting them calm me. I always felt at ease next to the ocean yet being in the water scared me. Something about swimming in deep water set me on edge and made my chest clench in terror.

I did not know how long I ran but my chest burned, and my legs ached. I stopped and put my hands behind my head, breathing in deep and letting it out gradually to slow my heart rate. I sat on the sand to rest for a moment and laid back, not caring if dirt got in my hair. The waves crashed against the shore and the sounds of the water lulled me into sleep.

At some point my body jolted awake. Momentary confusion caused my heart to race as I tried to figure out how I had gotten there. Ah, that's right, my mother wanted me to touch the fire. The sun was still high, telling me I hadn't been gone for long. I frowned as a sound caught my attention. I could hear someone singing but could not pinpoint where it was coming from. I listened closer, realizing it was the music that had woken me. I frowned in concentration and tilted my head forward trying to figure out if there were words in the song. It was a haunting melody full of pain and sadness. Tears stung my eyes and I wiped at them, staring down in confusion at the wetness on my hands. Why was I crying? The music cut off suddenly and I stood, trying to see if I could hear it again.

An object bobbing in the water made me forget about the song. It looked like a head, but it dipped under the water before I could get a good look. A moment later it reappeared, and I was sure it was a head this time.

My heart raced as panic set in. “Help!” I screamed, looking around for a lifeguard or someone who could help the drowning person.

The head bobbed back under the water. I ran to the edge of the ocean trying to find the person again, hoping that it was not too late. Water crashed against my legs, trying to push me back. The head surfaced again, and I noticed it was a young woman.

“Hold on!” I shouted to her.

I looked at the water, my chest tightening and a new kind of panic set in. I looked around one last time for anyone who could jump in and save the girl, but no one appeared. Biting my lip, I looked for the drowning girl then once I had her in my sights, I jumped in the water and swam to save her.

My chest clenched even more until it was hard to breathe. My flight instinct was in overdrive, but I ignored it. I ducked under an oncoming wave and resurfaced, trying to wipe the salty sea from my eyes and swim at the same time. I caught sight of the girl again, her haunting eyes and sad expression making me want to reach her faster. Why wasn’t she trying to swim? I pumped my arms through the water, racing to get to her side.

A large wave hit me in the face unexpectedly, sending me tumbling under water for a few seconds. I spluttered as I resurfaced, drawing in a lungful of air as I tried to regain my senses. I gagged at the taste of the ocean on my tongue which forced its way inside my mouth when the wave hit. I looked around the water for a floating head but found only choppy water.

Oh no! I lost the girl.

My head darted side to side, trying to find the drowning girl again. Was I too late?

"Hello? Can you hear me?" I called out, hoping the girl would answer.

I ducked under the water as another wave crashed over me but popped back up immediately. I could not find her anywhere. Suddenly, water rushed over me and into my mouth. I could not breathe. I could not find the surface. My sense of direction was all turned around. Starting to panic again, I kicked around in the water until my head finally burst through into open air only to be knocked under again by another wave.

I never had the chance to breathe in air before I was pushed under, so I was out of air and I was pretty sure I was crying since drowning was my greatest fear. Yeah, no way I would be getting over fear of water anytime soon. I felt like I was hallucinating, because I thought I heard music as I tumbled under the water.

The music got louder, and I realized it was the same song I heard on the beach. The song filled me with sadness again, making the tears fall harder, though the ocean swept them away. I felt drawn to the song and wanted to hear more. I drifted in the direction of the music wanting to dive deeper into the water to find its source. I shook my head to clear those thoughts. I needed to breathe! I swam in the opposite direction of the music and broke through the surface. I had enough time to breathe once before I was sucked under again.

This was it. I was going to die in the waters of Hawaii. At least my mom would know I was not blessed by a water myth. The song seemed closer now and something scaly darted by in my peripherals. If I wasn't surrounded by water, I was sure my face would be covered in salty tears from pain and fright. My lungs were burning, and darkness began to close in. The last thing I heard was the sorrowful music before I passed out and the last bit of air left my lungs.

My eyes snapped open and I drew in a deep lungful of air. I was back on the beach, laying on the sand and feeling…fine. I would have thought I dreamed the water experience except that my clothes were soaked. I grabbed a piece of my wavy, chestnut hair and examined it. I flung it behind me when I confirmed that it was also wet.

That means I did not dream the near-death experience. However, that did raise a ton of questions. How did I survive? Where was the girl in the water? What was that music I heard?

I needed to get back to the hotel and call for a search and rescue. I jumped up and raced back down the beach as fast as I could. When I saw the hotel, I ran faster, kicking up sand behind me.

I burst through the hotel doors, probably looking like a maniac, and shouted, “Help! Someone is drowning in the water!”

The hotel clerk picked up a phone and began speaking into it urgently. A few seconds later, a manager appeared with a walkie talkie and a few guys who I might have thought were athlete swimmers if they weren’t wearing logos for the search and rescue team.

“Where did you see this?” The manager asked with a calm voice.

I explained everything that happened, leaving out the part about hearing a strange song and led the manager and rescue team to the place I had almost drowned. My mother tagged along having heard my shouting in the hotel lobby and fretted over me.

I waited on the shore while the search team scouted the water for any traces of a body. I was starting to shiver but did not want to leave until I knew they found the woman. A blanket wrapped around me and I looked up to see my mother hugging me close. She rubbed my arms to warm me and made sure the blanket was tucked around me snuggly.

One of the rescue members jumped from a boat and into the water, disappearing for a few minutes. I stared confusingly at the water where he had gone waiting for him to resurface. He had been under there for quite some time. Looking around, I could see no one else was worried about the man so I waited.

Finally, I saw him shoot from the water like a dolphin and land gracefully on the boat deck. My eyes widened at the display. He must be myth blessed. I assumed either selkie or merman. I could not hear what they were saying but I saw the myth blessed man shake his head and look toward me.

Dread filled my stomach and fear started to make me shake. Did they find her body? What was wrong?

The manager's walkie talkie crackled and a voice from the boat sounded out of the device. "There was nothing there. The girl must have been mistaken."

I bristled. I most certainly was not mistaken. I saw a woman in the water more than once and almost lost my life trying to save her. The manager stared at me, waiting for an explanation.

"Sir, I would not lie about this. I saw a woman in the water right there," I pointed at a spot in the water, "and I even tried to swim after her."

The manager looked like he did not believe me, but he said calmly, "I will have them check a wider perimeter. You should head back to the hotel and rest." The manager looked at my mom, silent communication passing between them.

My mother gripped my shoulders and turned me around, leading us back to the hotel.

"I am not lying mom. I saw her in the water." I looked at her pleadingly, hoping she would believe me.

My mom rubbed my shoulders to comfort me. "I know honey, I know."

When we got back, my dad waited with coconut drinks in each hand. "Where did you two go?"

When he saw our expressions, his smile dropped. He handed my mother a drink then wrapped his free arm around my shoulders, guiding me to our room.

I waited hours for any news about the search. A knock on our door had me bolting to my feet and racing to answer it. My mom and dad were right behind me wanting to know what the search team found.

The manager of our hotel nodded in greeting and clasped his hands. "Hello. I wanted to let you know that the search team found no one under the water. Either they survived or there was no one there to begin with."

I started to argue that there was someone, but my father laid a hand on my shoulder, silencing me. "Thank you, sir."

The manager nodded and my dad closed the door. I turned to my parents with my arms outstretched. "I saw someone drowning, I swear!"

My dad patted my shoulder and gave me a smile that caused lines to appear around his chocolate brown eyes.

"Ok honey, we believe you. You heard the manager, maybe she survived and left the area."

I dropped my arms by my side and turned to the window looking out at the water. "Yeah, maybe. I hope so." I wasn't convinced but no amount of arguing would change anything.

For the rest of the trip, I refused to do any water related activities. My father suggested volcano tours, so I went on those, but the memory of the woman, the song, and my near-death experience kept me from enjoying Hawaii as much as I wanted to.

Eventually, it was time to leave the beautiful state and head back to the mountains of Colorado. I looked out the window on the plane at the Islands we were leaving behind and wondered what happened to the girl or if I did hallucinate the whole thing after all.

Chapter 2

Is My Singing That Bad?

A week passed since the near-death experience, meaning there was only one more week of summer break. Soon, I would have to start thinking about going back to school. I was excited to be spending senior year with my two best friends, who had also received negative results on their myth blessed test. However, I was dreading the looks my parents would be giving me since I was not going to Myth Blessed Academy.

As if it was my choice not to go.

I just had one more year, then I would be out of Colorado, away from my parents' disappointed and hopeful looks. I wanted to graduate then go to a university on the other side of the country and become a detective or an analyst. It did not matter where, as long as I was far away from Colorado. My parents usually told me not to think that far ahead whenever I spoke about my plans. According to them, I should wait to see what myth I was blessed by before choosing a profession. I gave an internal sigh at the thought.

"Hello!" Long slender fingers with purple nails snapped in front of my face.

I blinked and frowned at the owner of the fingers. "What?"

"We were asking if you wanted to go do karaoke," Tamara, one of my oldest and dearest friends, asked. She was crossing her arms and tapping her purple nails, waiting for my answer.

I had been too wrapped up in my thoughts, lately. Karaoke would be a fun way to get my mind off Hawaii and plans after graduation. I looked at my panda watch. It was only six, so my parents would be fine with it.

I played with the strap on my watch and shrugged. "Sure, I will go. But don't expect me to get up on stage. You know I am a horrible singer."

"Serena, you are not that bad!" Rae, my other oldest and dearest friend, exclaimed.

I glared at Rae's orange, poofy, short hair and round freckled face. "Remember what happened at your cousin's birthday party?"

Rae waved away the memory. "That glass was already cracked. It would have broken anyway."

"Yeah, and that time at the ski resort was not your fault either," Tamara said as she brushed her dark bangs aside.

I rolled my eyes. “Thanks for bringing that up again. I will go, but you cannot force me to get up there.” I crossed my arms in finality.

“Fiiiine,” Rae and Tamara said simultaneously.

I stood up, and opened the screen door, yelling into my house and hoping someone would hear me, “I’m going to Tang’s Karaoke with Rae and Tam!”

I waited for a response but did not get one. Oh well, they could text me if they were wondering where I was. My parents were usually cool with me going out as long as I let them know where I would be. I figured yelling into the house was fulfilling that agreement.

“C’mon! I want to get my hands on one of their pretzels!” Rae shouted from the car.

We hopped into Tamara’s midnight blue Jeep Cherokee and blasted music as we headed to Tang’s Karaoke. Every year at the end of summer, since we were ten years old, we would go to Tang’s. It was always a different experience because Tang changed his business every couple of years. One time it was an arcade. Another time it was an old-fashioned soda shop with ice cream. That one was my favorite. Now it was Karaoke. Last year was the beginning of his Karaoke business so I would not be surprised if Tang changed it next year.

We found a spot across the street in front of an old video store and piled out. We were able to cross the street easily since there were not a lot of cars passing by.

Historical downtown was neat, because most the streets were small and meant for walking or biking, making it difficult for cars to get around so no one usually tried.

"Oh, hello, hello!" Tang greeted us from behind the counter as we entered.

"Hello, Mr. Tang," Rae, Tam, and I called out and took seats at the counter.

"What can I get you girls?" Tang asked as he laid down a book of songs in front of us.

Tamara grabbed it and flipped through pages. She wrote down songs she wanted us to sing on a napkin and I felt nervous as the list grew.

"Three pretzels and a chocolate shake please," Rae ordered.

"Oh, make that two shakes," I added, "with a cherry."

Tang left to make our order. I looked around and noticed business was slow. There were a couple groups hanging around, and a man singing a screeching version of Sister Christian on stage, but otherwise it was empty. Thankfully, it wasn't long until food was placed in front of us.

"Alright, girls, here you go." Tang laid out our baskets of pretzels with delicious cheese sauce on the side and our milkshakes with whip cream and cherries on top.

Rae and I devoured our pretzels in a matter of minutes. Tang's pretzels were the absolute best because they were handmade, fresh, and huge. No matter what business he changed the place to, he always had pretzels for sale. We slowed down as we got halfway through our shakes and started looking over Tam's list of songs.

"I call this one," Rae said, pointing excitedly to a Faith Hill song.

Tamara and Rae divided the list up among the two of them until it was finally time to get up on stage. Tamara stood and walked over to the stage where she typed a song into the karaoke machine. The first notes of What a Girl Wants came over the speakers and Tam took a pose on stage waiting for the first lyrics. Rae and I got up and cheered by the front of the stage as Tamara's beautiful voice filled the room.

Tamara was by far the best singer I had ever met. Rae and I had urged her to go on America's Got Talent or American Idol, but she always refused. Rae was a good singer as well which she proved whenever she was on stage. Rae switched between rock and country songs while Tam stuck with classic pop but they both got everyone's attention every time.

After about the fifth or sixth song, Tam and Rae grabbed my arm, dragging me on stage. I tried to dig in my heel or make my body go limp, but they were annoyingly strong. A microphone was shoved into my hand as my best friends grinned at me. I pleaded with wide eyes to not make me sing, but they ignored me and started the song.

The first notes of My Heart Will Go On started and soon Rae was singing. "Every night in my dreams. I see you; I feel you. That is how I know you go on." Rae nodded at Tam.

Tam lifted the microphone to her mouth and sang the next verse, "Far across the distance. And spaces between us. You have come to show you go on."

Then it was my turn. I stared out at the tiny crowd, my heart beating furiously. Rae and Tam smiled at me encouragingly, waiting for me to sing the next notes. I did not have time to think, otherwise the moment would pass. I opened my mouth and sang the chorus, "Near, far, wherever you are. I believe that the heart does go on."

Rae and Tam joined in on the next part, our three voices blending perfectly. I sounded surprisingly good, and soon my fear washed away. I basked in the music, feeling as if there was nothing else in the world. I felt my soul open and pour out through my voice and the lyrics. I always did think this song was powerful and now I felt it touching everyone's hearts as I sang. Something tugged in my chest and I closed my eyes, feeling the song go through me and out of me into the crowd, drawing them in.

I noticed that Rae and Tam had stopped singing but I felt like I couldn't stop to find out why. I wanted to keep singing and finish the song. It was more than a want, it was a need. I needed to keep singing. The last notes rang out across the room and was I met with absolute silence. My euphoria from the moment faded and my self-consciousness reappeared. Was I that horrible at singing that no one wanted to clap? I had thought I did a decent job at not butchering the song but maybe I was wrong.

I looked at the crowd who stood near the stage, staring at me with blank fixed gazes, all with the same wide creepy smile. I couldn't tell whether they were happy or crazy. I looked to Rae and Tam to see what they thought. Rae stared at me with the same creepy stare and smile.

I walked over to my best friend and waved a hand in front of her face. "Rae? What's going on?"

I nearly jumped off the stage when a hand rested on my shoulder and a voice broke the silence in the room. "What did you do Serena?"

I looked at Tam's scared, hazel-gray eyes which most likely mirrored my own crystalline blue ones. "What do you mean? I didn't do this! Why are they like that? Why aren't we like that?" My voice rose as fear seeped into every part of my body.

Tam ignored me and pulled her phone with its glittery purple case from her pocket. She urgently tapped the screen with her long purple nails then held the phone up to her ear.

"Who are-" I started to ask.

Tam held up one slender finger telling me to hold on a minute. "Hello? Yes, this is Tamara of CO sector five.

I think we have a code blue." She waited as the person on the other side spoke. "Yes, Blue. Siren, I think." She paused again as the other person spoke. "Ok, Tang's Karaoke in downtown. See you soon." She hung up and put the phone back in her pocket.

"Tamara Abdala, you better start speaking now," I said slowly and forcefully.

Tam held up her hands to show she meant no harm. "Hold on, Serena. I will explain." She glanced at the crowd behind me, slight fear shining in her eyes. "You've gotta calm down."

I glanced behind me and noticed the crowd had moved in closer and were now frowning although they still smiled widely. It was disturbing and sent shivers down my arms.

"What's wrong with them?" I asked, turning back to Tam. "Who did you call?"

Tam let out a deep breath and put her hands on her head, glancing at Rae then back to me. "This was never supposed to happen. Your tests were negative. How did this happen?"

I gripped her arms, forcing her to put them back to her side. "Hey, Tam, stay focused. Who did you call?"

Tam ignored my question and stared into my eyes with worry and a crease between her eyebrows. "I thought you weren't myth blessed Serena."

I stepped back at her words. "Wha-I-I'm not," I stammered.

Tam snorted in disbelief and waved out at the crowd and at Rae. "I think you are."

I looked out over the crowd, disbelief trying to overpower the growing realization that I did in fact do something to them. I felt it when I was singing. A connection and a tug in my chest pulling in the crowd through the music. What kind of mythological creature could do that?

I must have said the last part out loud because Tamara answered softly beside me, "A siren."

Before I could comment on that, the doors burst open and three figures walked in. The man leading the charge looked to be in his fifties with salt and pepper hair and a stubbly beard but somehow still looked handsome. The other two were younger, maybe around my age. One was a tall girl with long, flowing, ultra-light blonde hair, a sweet yet dangerous look in her aqua eyes, and holding a silver dagger. The last stranger was a tall guy, just a bit taller than the dagger holding girl, with broad shoulders, short, black spiky hair and a scowl that could cause terror in any soul. A movement by their feet drew my attention to a frightening sight. A giant lizard stood by them, analyzing the room with an eerie intelligence.

"Tamara Abdala?" The older man asked stepping forward.

Tam stepped down from the stage and walked over to the three scary newcomers, greeting each of them in turn yet keeping her distance from the large lizard. I stayed where I was and glanced at the back exit, wondering if I should make a break for it.

"Can you help us fix them?" Tam asked the girl.

The mysterious girl glanced at me from across the room. I felt a weird connection to her from deep within, but I did not know how since I had never seen her before in my life.

"Of course, I can," the girl sneered and pushed her way passed Tam to stand in front of the enchanted crowd.

The older man took out a set of ear plugs and handed a pair to the scowling guy. Once they had the plugs in their ears, the leader gave a nod to the girl. She started singing, softly at first but intensified it as she continued. That connection from within tugged at my chest, drawing me to the song and to her. I jerked back in surprise when I realized it was the same song I heard in Hawaii from the water. How was that possible?

Without realizing it, I had stepped down from the stage and stood in front of her. Noise from behind me made me turn around and my eyes widened at the sight of the crowd rousing from their trance. They didn't seem to notice that they were even in one. This girl must be siren blessed…like me. That was a difficult thought to wrap my mind around.

Poor Rae seemed lost on stage, wondering where we went. Finally, she spotted us, and frowned in confusion at the people we were with as she walked over to us.

"What's going on?" Rae asked.

A bubble of laughter rose up and escaped me. The strangers and my friends stared at me, but more laughter kept bubbling up. This situation was crazy! I wanted to know what was going on, too. Who were these mysterious people?

"I think we better take this somewhere else. Please follow me." The older man turned and walked out of Tang's Karaoke. I glanced at Tam and a confused Rae before following the strangers outside.

We gathered around a small table that was set outside with an umbrella over it. Tam, Rae, the leader, and I took seats while the other two stood by with crossed arms. The two standing people kept glaring at each other. There was some kind of history there, but I didn't have the time or energy to figure it out.

"Can someone please tell me what is going on?" I asked my palms sweaty and dread twisting my insides.

The leader glanced at Rae with suspicion and hesitation, but Tam nodded letting him know it was okay to talk in front of her. The leader nodded in understanding and held out a hand in greeting. "Well, first off I am Dominic Drakari, Principal of the Myth Blessed Academy of Colorado."

My eyes widened as I took his hand and shook it. "Serena Carter."

"Myth Blessed Academy? Why are you here?" Rae asked surprised and looked around to find the myth blessed person he must be there to meet.

I shifted in my seat and struggled to meet their eyes. "I, um, kinda did something myth-y."

Rae stared at me with an open mouth and wide eyes. "What'd you do?"

Dominic sidestepped the question and introduced the other two. "This is Laneli Michaels, siren blessed, Elliot Maganot, dragon blessed, and his familiar, Moto."

Rae and I sucked in a surprised breath. Being Dragon blessed was rare. In order to be blessed by a mythological creature, you had to have been around one at some point in your life. Dragons have not been recorded in ages so the fact that he was blessed by one was amazing yet frightening.

I didn't get a chance to ask Elliot about being dragon blessed, what a familiar was or why it was a giant lizard because Dominic drew our attention back to him. "Serena, what you did cannot happen again. Without knowing the full extent of your gifts, you might hurt someone."

I looked down at the table guiltily. "How was I supposed to know I could do that? Aren't your tests supposed to pick up on that?"

It was his turn to look guilty. "Well, yes. I don't know why your tests came back negative. Either way, we know now. You must attend Myth Blessed Academy as soon as possible."

He produced an envelope from inside his coat pocket and handed it to me. I stared down at the stamp of the school crest and the big letters saying Myth Blessed Academy. I knew going up on that stage would be a bad idea. I just never knew it would turn out like this. At least my parents would be happy. They finally got a myth blessed daughter.

I opened the envelope, reading it over carefully while Tam and Rae squeezed in to read over my shoulder. Apparently, I would be starting Myth Blessed Academy the following day.

Dominic Drakari followed me home to talk to my parents and explained that Laneli would be staying with me until then to make sure I did not use my powers accidentally. Drakari did not even ask if it was okay for her to stay, but it would not have mattered. My parents were way too excited and would have agreed to anything.

"Our daughter is a siren! Oh my! We should have guessed," My mother said excitedly to my father.

I feel like she would have said that no matter what mythological creature I was blessed by. They sure did try to cover everything when they tested me in their own way. I shuddered, thinking about some of the lengths they went to test me.

Laneli cleared her throat to get my mom's attention. "She is not a siren. She is blessed by one."

My mother waved away her words and whispered excitedly to my dad who was smiling proudly as if it was his blessing that made me that way. I left them talking to themselves and walked over to sit by Laneli on the couch.

"So, what should I expect tomorrow?" I did not want to meet her eyes, so I stared at my shoes as I kicked them side to side.

"You will be given a class schedule and a dorm room-"

I interrupted her, "Dorm room? So, I will be staying there all day every day?"

"Yes, did you expect to have to travel that kind of distance every day?" She asked with a raised thin eyebrow.

I deflated. "I guess not." That just meant I wouldn't be able to see my friends as much. Something from earlier came back to me. "Why did Tamara call you guys? How did she even have your number? How did you get there so fast?"

Laneli looked uncomfortable, which contradicted her usual confident air. "I don't know if I am the one who should tell you about your friend, but the way we got there was from the powers of another myth blessed at the Academy."

I wondered what kind of myth blessed had the powers to send people far distances in a short amount of time. I would have to come back to that later. “Fine.” I decided not to push the Tamara topic and put a mental pin in it. I would wring the truth from Tam if I had to later. “What will school be like?”

Laneli’s confident posture came back as we returned to a safer topic. “Well, you will probably have a roommate of the same element as you, meaning a water type, and you will have classes that teach you about our history and abilities mixed in with your common classes.”

“Water type?” I asked. I feel like I had heard about this at school a bit but could not remember the details.

I thought I saw Laneli roll her eyes but couldn’t be sure. “Every mythological creature is put into one of five elements. Since you are siren blessed, and sirens are of the water, then you are a water type.”

I nodded slowly, but still did not quite understand. “What does our elements have to do with anything?”

Laneli took a deep breath before answering, as if trying to hold on to her patience. “Usually the myth blessed have a small affinity for the element of which they are blessed from.”

I wanted to ask more about affinities and elements, but I could tell she was getting annoyed with my questions. I couldn’t help but ask one more though, as my memories of Hawaii resurfaced. "Have you ever seen a real siren?"

Laneli looked at me, studying me as if trying to see what the real meaning was behind the question. "No. I've never seen one, or any mythological creature for that matter." She sounded guarded but then again, I didn't know her well enough to know that for sure.

I was starting to wonder if the woman I saw in the water in Hawaii was actually a siren. It would make so much sense, but since Laneli couldn't tell me what one looked like I had no idea if my guess was correct.

"Well, I guess I better start packing." I got up and walked to my room, closing the door securely behind me.

I leaned against the door and slumped, thinking about the night's events. I put a room full of people into a trance by singing. My best friend was somehow not affected and had Dominic Drakari's number in her phone. I would be going to a school built for teaching people like me. My life had changed, and I did not know whether it was for the better or worse.

Chapter 3

The Academy

A black SUV with tinted windows and the Myth Blessed Academy crest stamped on the side waited for Laneli and I the next morning. I was sure my neighbors were wondering what that car was doing in front of my house and would be gossiping soon enough. If word did not get around through my neighbors, I was sure my mother and father would be blabbing about it as soon as I left.

I took my two suitcases and small duffle bag over to the vehicle where the driver took them and placed them in the back. My parents left the porch and walked over with their arms wide open.

"Have fun at your new school honey," my dad said, giving me a crushing hug.

My mom stepped forward next and gave me a softer hug and a kiss on the head. "I always knew you were blessed. Now do your best in school and take as many pictures as you can."

I gave her a frown but did not comment. She just wanted pictures to show to her friends. That was what all this was about. Being Myth Blessed would help me get jobs easier since anyone would be lucky to have someone with abilities on their team, but my mom was always wanting the prestige and attention having a myth blessed child would bring.

I waved to my parents and got in the SUV, glad that the windows were tinted so they wouldn't see the tears building in my eyes. I should be excited that this opportunity has risen but my life changed overnight, and all my hopes and plans would change with it. I was no longer the same Serena Carter, and that fact was going to give me a bad case of identity crisis.

The drive was about an hour long since the Academy was near Denver, more specifically in a section of Roxborough State Park. I had visited the park once before, when I was thirteen years old, but we were not able to get close to the school. We would get as close as possible and my mom would point in the direction of the Academy, telling me I would end up there one day. Looks like she was right. The State park was beautiful, with red rock formations and trees that contrasted nicely with the colors in the rocks. Now I guess I would be living there for a year.

The car traveled along winding dirt roads until it came up to a massive metal gate with the school crest on the front. The driver held out a badge to the guard who looked it over before handing it back and waving us through.

Beyond the gates was a massive green field and stone paths leading in all directions. I could see people, students I presumed, walking along some of them. The students looked so normal, but I didn't know what I was expecting otherwise. Wings or horns, maybe. The car pulled up alongside the entrance to the school and the driver got out to open our doors. When I stepped out, I took a moment to look around and was secretly impressed by what I saw.

A massive school that reminded me of an English palace stood in front of me. Turning in a slow circle, I could see the paths and green lawn that I saw from the car. Off to the right of the school was a small building that upon asking about I discovered was a stable. I had never ridden a horse but the fact that I had the choice now sent thrills through me. On the other side of the school was a large garden with more flowers than I have ever seen in one place. Various trees stood among the lawn and within the garden as well.

"I will take you to Mr. Drakari's office," Laneli said, seeming a bit bored.

I looked back at the driver who got into the car and started to drive away. "What about my luggage?"

"Someone will have it brought to your dorm room." Laneli walked away not waiting for a response.

I quickly caught up with her before I got lost and looked around in awe at the inside of the school. High vaulted ceilings, marble columns, decorated walls and floors. Students walking in pairs or groups stared at me as we passed and started whispering. I didn't want to look like a nervous, scared new girl so I straightened my shoulders and looked ahead, trying to show confidence.

We took a couple turns and walked down long halls, eventually stopping at a door with a name on the front reading D. Drakari.

"Here you go. I guess I will see you around." Again, Laneli walked away without waiting for a response.

I took a deep breath beforc entering the principal's office. His office seemed more like a study with bookshelves full of books, some ancient looking, and a mahogany desk. He was sitting behind his desk looking at an open book as he took notes in a journal next to it. He did not notice my entrance, so I cleared my throat to get his attention.

Mr. Drakari looked up from his notes and smiled at me. He was wearing a long-sleeved black turtleneck and glasses. "Ah, there you are." He leaned over and pulled out a drawer from his desk. "I have your schedule right here."

He handed me a folded paper and I tucked it away. I would look at it later once I had a chance to settle in. He handed me another piece of paper, this one thicker.

"That's the map of the school. I went ahead and starred your classes and circled your room," Drakari said, pointing to the map in my hands. "Here, I will go ahead and take you to the water wing."

"Water wing?" I asked following him out into the hallway.

Drakari turned right and started walking down the hall. "We have five dorm buildings here, one for each of the elements. Some mythological creatures are part of two elements, so we do our best to place everyone in the best dorm."

"How can myths be part of two elements?" I asked, trying to understand the element system at the school. Laneli mentioned it last night but I was still confused.

Drakari opened a set of double doors and led us outside. We seemed to be in the back of the school now. "Take me for example. I am werewolf blessed meaning I am of the spirit and earth."

I nodded slowly but still did not understand.

Catching my confused expression Drakari chuckled and stopped. "Don't worry, there is a beginner's class for that stuff that I added to your list of classes. You are going to be very busy."

I finally looked up at our surroundings and saw five smaller buildings, yet large enough to house probably fifty people each, situated in a semicircle facing the school. A large grass lawn stretched from the school to the dorms and everything was surrounded by trees.

"That one is the earth wing," Drakari explained, pointing to one of the buildings nearest the forest. His hand moved to point to the one directly next to it, "That one is the air wing."

I looked at the next building that was standing in front of a large lake. "I'm guessing that one is where I will be staying?" I asked and nodded my head to the building in the middle of the five.

"Yes, and the other two are spirit and fire," Drakari finished pointing at the last two. He leaned over and whispered, "we had to separate water and fire because of a long-standing rivalry."

"Rivalry?" I looked between the fire and water buildings. You wouldn't be able to tell there was a rivalry just by looking at the identical wings.

"Yes, unfortunately fire and water do not mix, and the students have taken it a bit too seriously." Drakari shook his head at the drama that must have caused him many headaches then walked across the lawn heading for the water wing.

I walked beside him and soon we were entering the water wing. I expected aquariums or fountains to showcase the water aspect of the water wing, but I was met with only a plain sitting room and long bland halls branching off in four directions. He guided me up two flights of stairs until we were on the third floor. Great, I had to deal with stairs.

Drakari stopped in front of room 304. "Alright, this is where you will be staying. Do you think you will be able to find it again?"

I nodded. "Yeah, I think so."

"Good. Your roommate can show you around a bit. Your classes will start in the morning."

Before I could ask about why my classes started on a Wednesday, he was already descending the stairs. I sighed and turned back to the door of my new home. Should I knock?

I gave a light double tap on the door before opening it slowly. I never had a roommate before, so I didn't know what to expect.

The room was spacious with two twin sized beds on either side of the room, a dresser at the end of each bed and two desks side by side against the window which I was pleased to see looked out over the lake. A squeal had me turning in time to be crushed by a small child.

"Hi, I was so excited when I heard I would be getting a roommate!" The girl was around my age but was only about five feet tall and had brown pigtails tied with ribbons.

I stumbled back when her skin became clear and blue as if she were made of water then went back to normal.

"Oops, sorry, I do that when I am excited." She beamed at me and held out a hand. "I'm Marion."

I slowly took her hand and shook it, expecting to pass through it as I would in water. “I’m Serena. Um, what, uh, mythological creature blessed you if you don’t mind me asking?”

Marion kept up her cheery tone and popped around the room, cleaning things up. “I’m sprite blessed.”

An image of a Sprite can filled with bubbly, carbonated soda touching Marion’s head with an angelic light surrounding her filled my mind. Somehow, I didn’t think that was what she meant. “What is a sprite?”

“Well the one that I was blessed by was a water sprite, a spirit of the water, almost like a fairy but not as solid.” She jumped in front of me. “And you are siren blessed right?”

I guessed that was why she had a not-so-solid body sometimes. “Uh, yeah, I guess I’m siren blessed though I am new to it. Wait, so if a water sprite is a spirit but lives in the water…”

“Yup! That means I have an affinity with the spirit and water elements, though water is stronger which is why I live in this dorm.” Her attention shifted to something behind me. “Ooo, do you want me to help you unpack?” She ran over to the other side of the room making me turn to keep her in sight.

She stood by my bags near the other bed that must now be mine. “No, I think I can manage.”

“Alrighty! Ooo, what are your classes?” She asked excitedly.

She seemed to not be able to sit still as she flitted around the room and jumped from one topic to another. I was starting to think she had ADHD or something.

I pulled out my class schedule and handed it over to her. I left her studying it and walked over to my bags to start unpacking. It had only been about a couple hours, but I was already feeling homesick.

“Figured that one, interesting, yes, mhm, ick, aww you have Laneli, boo,” Marion mumbled as she looked over my schedule.

“What’s wrong with Laneli? She seemed okay when I met her.” I grabbed a stack of socks and walked over to the dresser to dump them into a drawer.

“Nothing too bad. She is just, mmm, how do I put this, a drama queen. She thinks she owns the water wing and is the main antagonist in the water-fire rivalry. Her and that dragon blessed guy.” Marion shook her head in annoyance but gave me a bright smile that contradicted her words.

“Do you mean Elliot?” My interest was piqued since I happened to meet the two people Marion mentioned yesterday.

Marion rolled her eyes. “Ugh, yes. Don’t let his good looks fool you. He is dangerous and hates all water elementals.” Marion walked over to my bed and flopped onto it, handing back my schedule in the process. “Enough about them. How about I give you a tour, it is almost lunch.”

My stomach grumbled. “Yeah, thanks, I am getting pretty hungry. Wait, don’t you have classes you should be at?”

Marion let out a tinkling laugh, reminding me of a fairy. Or a water sprite, I guessed. “They let me skip today so I could show you around.”

We walked out into the hall and down the stairs until we were standing in front of the building. “Did Mr. Drakari already explain the dorms?” Marion asked looking at the semicircle of buildings.

“Yeah he said that one over there by the forest is the earth wing, then air, ours, spirit and fire.” I was pleased I remembered.

Marion took me around to the back of the water wing. “Right. Let me show you our lake. It is the most amazing thing and every water myth blessed seems to have an instant connection to it. Some people say naiads used to live in the lake.”

My brows scrunched as I tried to remember the mythology of naiads. “Aren’t naiads bound forever to whatever water source they were born in?”

Marion put a finger on her lips and looked out over the water, looking for the answer. “I think so.”

“But you said, ‘used to live.’ What happened to them?” I looked at the glittering blue lake and wondered if there were naiads like she said.

Marion shrugged. “I also said ‘some people say’ so it could be a legend or something. I’ve never seen any.”

She led me down to the lake and crouched by the water's edge reaching a hand into it. Marion's skin turned clear again, and she seemed to be drawing energy from the water. She reached out and yanked the water up until it was standing upright in front of us.

"Whoa, how'd you do that?" I asked in wonder.

For some reason, I was not afraid of the display. I reached out to the standing water but paused before my skin touched it. Who knew what magical water would do to a person? It continued flowing in the same vertical column before Marion let go and it splashed back into the lake.

"I can control water, although I am not very skilled." Marion studied me for a moment. "Come here and dip your hand in the water."

My nerves instantly flared, and I took a step back. "I don't know about that. I think I am fine standing here." The lake turned from peaceful to frightening in a second.

Marion leaned forward and grabbed my hand, pulling me to the edge. "It's not going to hurt you, just touch the water."

She was right. I don't know why I was freaking out. We were not going all the way into the lake. It was only the edge. Images of my near-death experience surfaced in my mind, but I shook them away and leaned down. Slowly I put my hand in the water and felt…nothing. I was expecting some kind of powerful feeling or energy, but it was just water.

I looked into Marion's excited and expectant eyes. What was she expecting to happen? Her smile dimmed a bit, and a confused frown creased her forehead, but she hid it by turning and walking back to the lawn, calling me to follow her. She was surprisingly quick for someone so small. I ran after her and let her take me on the rest of the tour, figuring she would explain to me about the lake eventually.

I was shown the location of the classrooms that I would need to find again tomorrow, the garden, stables, an outside training area almost like a gym, the library, and finally the cafeteria. Smells of delicious food wafted from the cafeteria when we neared it causing my stomach to grumble. I had been too nervous to eat breakfast that morning, so I was running on empty.

Marion let out a tinkling laugh at my stomach noises and guided me into the room. The cafeteria looked cozy with stone walls, an actual fireplace, and tables set up around the room.

She led the way through the short line. I was surprised and highly pleased to see an assortment of appetizing food. I grabbed some fruit, pizza, a yogurt and Sprite and followed Marion to a nearby table that gave us a view of the room.

As we ate, Marion pointed out certain groups of people eating in the room. I did not know why I was surprised to find cliques in that school. We all may be myth blessed, but we were still teenagers. I saw Laneli with two other girls who looked almost identical to her sitting at a central table. Another table held some of the more powerful air and earth myths and I noticed two of them had birds perched on their arms. A couple others held smaller animals on their lap. There was a table with students who wore all black and glared at anyone who came near them. Apparently, they were spirit blessed who happened to be closer to darkness such as vampires and wendigos. Marion pointed out the fire group with a missing Elliot. One of the students in the fire group had a ferret and another had a dog by their side. I blinked in surprise when I took a closer look and discovered the dog was truly a fox. Before I could ask about it someone dropped a tray on our table.

The stranger had short curly black hair, darker skin, a small scar near his eye, and glasses. The most noticeable part that was hard to look away from was the eagle perched on his shoulder. He leaned over and kissed Marion on her cheek, not seeming fazed by the large bird.

Marion blushed, turning clear for a second like I saw her do earlier in our room. “This is Devon.”

Devon flashed a set of perfect white teeth and waved in greeting.

I gave Devon a small wave. "I'm Serena, Marion's new roommate." My eyes were drawn back to the bird that no one had mentioned yet.

"Oh! So, this is her," Devon said to Marion with interest.

Marion nodded excitedly.

Since no one was explaining I decided to ask. "Why do you have an eagle on your shoulder? And while we are on the subject of animals, why are there animals in the cafeteria, like that fox?" I asked pointing to the fox at the fire table.

"You haven't told her about familiars?" Devon asked Marion astonished.

Marion shrugged, looking guilty, but Devon was the one to explain. "Some myth blessed people have more power than others. When that happens, an animal usually becomes bonded to them, traditionally one having to do with their myth, that helps them channel and control the power. This here is Gus."

I remembered the large lizard that stood by Elliot last night. Moto was Elliot's familiar then, meaning Elliot must be powerful if I was understanding correctly. That also meant Devon had a lot of power. I wondered how an animal could help control and channel the power inside.

"What myth are you blessed by?" I asked Devon but stared at Gus the eagle.

“Griffin,” Devon answered with a mouth full of his sandwich.

I knew griffins had the body of a lion and the head and wings of an eagle, so Gus made sense as his familiar. I looked between Marion and Devon. I assume a Griffin is of the air element, so how did Marion and Devon meet? I probably shouldn’t pry into other people’s business, so I stayed quiet and ate the rest of my food.

The doors to the cafeteria crashed open causing total silence in the room. Elliot with a frown in place and Moto with a slithering tongue stood in the doorway searching the room. His eyes locked on to someone from across the room, his frown deepening as he stalked forward with clenched fists.

“Uh oh, here we go. I didn’t think you would see this so soon, but I should’ve known better,” Marion said shaking her head.

“See what?” I asked glancing briefly at Marion before looking at Elliot’s furious stalking again.

Marion pointed at Elliot silently telling me to watch.

Elliot and Moto stalked toward the table where Laneli and the two other blonde girls were sitting. “You’ve taken this too far,” Elliot growled.

“Whatever do you mean?” Laneli blinked innocently up at him.

“You know you are not allowed to use your enchantment outside of class! Making them stand outside in their underwear was uncalled for!" Elliot shouted with clenched fists. Moto hissed and sidled closer to Laneli.

Marion whistled low under her breath. My eyebrows rose at the image of Laneli singing and putting some guys in a trance. I didn't know we could tell people to do things while they were in that trance.

Laneli stood along with her two companions. "I don't know what you mean." Laneli's smirk contradicted her words.

A fireball formed in Elliot's hands, and black scales erupted over parts of his skin, but Laneli didn't back down. Before either one could do anything, Mr. Drakari was there standing in between them. I didn't even see him come into the room.

"Back down, Elliot." Mr. Drakari stared into Elliot's eyes, not even glancing at the fireball.

Elliot glared past Drakari at Laneli but extinguished the fireball. His scales slowly disappeared until he looked like a normal human.

"Both of you, my office now." Drakari waited until the two started moving in the direction of the exit before breaking out of his stance.

The three of them left causing the silence to end. Groups chatted excitedly among themselves, discussing the new drama that unfolded.

I turned to Marion and Devon. "Are they always like that?"

Marion shrugged. “Pretty much.”

Chapter 4

First Day

The next day, I had to wake up around seven to get to my first class on time which was myth history. I had already learned some of the basic history about how mythological beings blessed human children, in turn giving them some of their special abilities. Mr. Drakari found it necessary for me to take the beginner class anyway.

Marion had been at Myth Blessed Academy for four years already, so she was in the last year of her schooling. That meant she didn't have any classes until eleven. Lucky.

I left my room quietly so I would not disturb Marion and walked down the stairs into the quad and toward the school. Once I was inside, I noticed only a handful of students were going to class this early. Pulling my map out, I studied it as I walked down the halls looking for

Professor Jamens' class. I frowned, turning the map around to see if I was holding it correctly and turned down another hallway. My body hit something hard causing me to stumble back and drop the map.

"I'm sorry," I said, bending down to retrieve my map. When I stood back up, I looked into fiery copper eyes. "Oh, Elliot, um, hi." Smooth Serena.

He grunted and crossed his arms in acknowledgement of my greeting. He needed better conversation skills.

"So, what are you doing here?" I asked, trying to get him to talk to me. I didn't want the water-fire feud to involve me, so I was trying to go for polite and friendly.

One dark eyebrow rose telling me it should be obvious. That, or he was trying to say it was none of my business. It's not like I speak the language of Elliot's eyebrows.

"Right, it's a school, and you're a student so you're probably trying to go to class. Or you are coming back from class. Either way it is school related. Unless you were just walking through the halls for non-school related reasons," I babbled.

Elliot's other dark brow rose to meet his first one, and he gave me an amused look.

"Um, anyway, I got to go. Bye!" I quickly walked around him.

Halfway down the hall I found my classroom. I glanced behind me before going inside and saw Elliot standing in the same spot, staring at me curiously. I ducked into the class, finding a seat near the front, and shook my head to clear the memory of that embarrassing non-conversation. Next time I needed to be less awkward. A moment later, Professor Jamens called our attention and began our class. I fought to cool my heated cheeks and focus on my teacher.

Classes at Myth Blessed Academy started on Monday, so I had missed two days. Thankfully, they were still beginning, so I had not missed much. Mr. Jamens was kind enough to recap what they went over the last couple of days by asking the students to explain the history.

Mr. Jamens started the discussion, "What happened about seventy years ago?"

A young boy, around thirteen, raised his hand from the second row. When Mr. Jamens nodded at him, the boy explained, "World War II, which threatened not only the human world but also the mythological world."

"Right. What was the effect?" Jamens asked, crossing his arms.

A girl, also around thirteen, raised her hand but spoke before Jamens could call on her. "Mythological beings decided to add their own help to the war but coming out of hiding was not a good idea due to the history of being hunted, so the mythological beings decided to bless the humans with their gifts giving the allies an advantage in the war."

Jamens smiled proudly at the class. “Right again. Since then, the myths have been blessing children so they may grow up to help protect our world.”

I had heard about the blessings originating around World War II, but I never heard about the mission Myth Blessed students had weighing on their shoulders. Protect the world? How were we supposed to do that?

“Alright, now that we are all caught up,” Mr. Jamens glanced briefly at me, “we will continue our unit on water myths. We will talk about the myth, origin, and geography of selkies today.”

A guy in the back of class clapped making me assume he was selkie blessed. I was intrigued by the topic and history. If every day was like that then myth history may become my favorite.

Soon, Mr. Jamens was calling the end to class and wishing us a great day as we shuffled out. I looked at my schedule to see my next class then the map to see where I needed to go. It was not too hard to get to. I went back down the hall then up the stairs to the third floor. Thankfully, I would be up there most of the time so I would not have to trek back and forth to each floor.

My next three classes were okay though they were nothing special. After my fourth class of the day, it was finally lunch. I made my way downstairs to the cafeteria, hoping I remembered where it was located. I felt confident enough that I didn’t use my map but soon, unfamiliar corridors began to surround me. I stopped after the third unfamiliar corridor and turned around in a slow circle. Where was I? If I got lost, then I would not be able to eat since I would have to go to class. Letting out a frustrated sigh, I pulled out my map and glanced down trying to figure out where I was.

A throat cleared behind me, drawing my attention. I turned around to find a guy with dark clothing and shoulder length hair of the darkest color I had ever seen. It was like onyx wrapped in shadows. I blinked realizing his whole body seemed to be cloaked in actual shadows.

"You lost?" The stranger asked.

"Uh, yeah." I shook my head feeling rude for staring at his shadows and looked back at the map. "I am trying to find the cafeteria."

The guy chuckled. "You are going the wrong way."

"I figured that much out," I joked.

"I will take you there." He stepped closer, peering at the map and pointed to a spot on it. "This is where we are now."

My eyes widened. "How did I get so far away!"

A smile broke out on his face and I nearly gasped. I was not usually into goth looking guys but my goodness that smile could change my preferences quickly.

"Follow me." The stranger seemed to glide as he guided me along.

I kept glancing at him, curious about what myth he was blessed by. I didn't realize I was staring again until he cleared his throat. "What's wrong?"

“Oh! Uh, nothing.” I decided to change the topic before I embarrassed myself more. “I’m Serena.”

The shadow guy nodded but didn’t offer any comment or greeting.

A few seconds of silence passed. If this guy was going for dark and mysterious, he was doing a good job. I broke the silence by asking, “So, what is your name?”

Silence descended again. I wasn’t sure if he heard me, but I didn’t want to ask again in case he was not answering on purpose. Maybe his threshold for politeness ended at helping girls who were lost.

Eventually we reached the cafeteria doors, which I knew because for one we stopped, and two the smells hit me causing my stomach to grumble. I really needed to get my stomach under control.

“Well, thank you, um, stranger.” I waved, starting to walk toward the doors.

His hand flashed out of his shadows and gripped my hand, pulling me back. Surprised, I let out a squeak and caught my balance just before I fell against him.

He raised my hand to his lips and gave it a small kiss. “I’m Harvey.”

I looked at him with wide eyes, too shocked to comment. A moment later, Harvey vanished with only a trace of shadows left behind leaving me speechless by the cafeteria doors. I blinked, trying to figure out what was more important to focus on. The kiss on my hand or the shadowy vanishing act.

I walked into the cafeteria dazed, wanting to find Marion to ask her about the odd yet intriguing stranger. I found her at the table we were sitting at the day before, leaning close to Devon and giggling.

I dropped down on the other side startling them both. "I just met the most…I don't know person."

Gus flapped his wings to gain his balance from being startled at my sudden appearance then settled on Devon's shoulder again calmly.

"How very descriptive," Marion joked giving me a curious look.

"His name was Harvey. I got lost and he helped me find my way here. He disappeared like that." I snapped my fingers to show how fast he disappeared.

Marion nodded her head but frowned. "Harvey is a curious individual I will say that. He was the one to send Mr. Drakari to you that night. There are tons of rumors going around about that guy, though."

He was the one who sent Drakari to the Karaoke place? I would ask about that later. I frowned, feeling defensive of a guy I barely met. "They're just rumors though, right?"

Devon tilted his head side to side, indicating I could be correct, but I could also be wrong. "I have heard he hides in the shadows and scares people."

"I heard he hides in the shadows of people's rooms and gives them nightmares," Marion added.

"Someone said once that Harvey broke all the bones in a guy's body in gym just by reaching out and crushing his shadow," Devon whispered.

I shook my head in disbelief. Even though I had only been around him for a brief time, that kiss on my hand made him seem gentle and his aloofness made me think he would rather stay out of people's business.

I shrugged. "I don't know if I believe any of that."

Marion and Devon shrugged back. "You can believe whatever you want, we are only telling you what we heard," Marion said.

I nodded in understanding. The bell sounded overhead, and I groaned. I still hadn't eaten. I looked at Marion and Devon's tray. "You going to eat that?" I pointed to an apple on Marion's tray.

She shook her head and chuckled, handing me the fruit. I took it, eating it as I walked out to my next class. This time I had to go outside, off to the side of the school, for gym class.

My classmates were standing in a circle, so I pushed through to stand next to a couple of people, facing the coach. The coach saw me and marked something on his clipboard then looked at his watch. No one said anything for a couple of minutes. I looked around, trying to see if I was missing something. Were they waiting on me? My question was answered when somebody pushed into the circle to stand by my side.

“Finally, everyone is here,” coach said annoyed and marked his clipboard again.

I looked to my side to see Elliot. I was both surprised and intrigued that he was in my class. He was avoiding my gaze, but I knew he saw my curious stare. I looked around us but didn’t see Moto. Where was his giant lizard?

“Line up!” Coach called, waving his hand in the air.

I moved with everyone else to stand in a straight line facing the coach. My neck tingled when hot breath blew onto it as the person beside me spoke near my ear.

“Make sure not to bump into anyone,” Elliot whispered.

I turned to glare at Elliot for bringing up our interaction earlier that day. His face was blank so I couldn’t tell if he was joking with me or making fun of me. I faced forward, deciding to ignore him but I was still highly aware of his presence. I never realized it before, but he had a strong heat, like fire, coming from him and he smelled like a campfire.

“I want you all to run to that fence and back. Before we do any self-defense or combat training, you need to build up cardio!” The coach shouted at us.

I never understood why coaches felt the need to shout all the time. The coach blew his whistle, and everyone sprinted toward the fence. I was okay with running. In fact, I liked running when I wanted to get away and clear my head, however I was probably the least fit person there.

I made it to the fence alright but on the way back I started wheezing and slowing down. Everyone darted passed me until I was the only one still running. Finally, I crossed the line and stopped, putting my hands behind my head to breathe better. I looked up to see Elliot smirking at me with his arms crossed. I scowled at him and walked to the other side of the class, separating his smirking face from my lack of athletic skill.

For the rest of class, the coach had us doing cardio workouts until most of us were collapsed and sweating buckets. I was annoyed to see Elliot standing, looking calm and energized after all that. When the coach called the end of class everyone dispersed. Elliot was gone in a flash, apparently not wanting to be there a second longer than necessary. I took my time to get up and walk to the lake for my tutoring session. I wanted to look like I wasn't dying by the time I got there.

I saw Laneli kneeling by the water with her eyes closed looking at peace. I knelt beside her making sure to make a noise as I sat down, so she knew I was there, but Laneli didn't stir.

"Hi, Laneli, I don't know if you remember me, but-" I started.

"Shh," Laneli interrupted.

I closed my mouth. How long would we have to be quiet? This seemed more like meditation than tutoring. I looked out over the glittering lake. It was truly beautiful, especially with the red mountains and trees around it. A movement in the water caught my attention. For a second, I thought I saw eyes and long hair, but it was gone in an instant.

"Do you feel the connection to the water?" Laneli asked, drawing my attention to her.

I looked at the lake again, waiting to feel something within me, but like yesterday I felt nothing. "No."

Laneli finally opened her eyes to look at me with her crystal blue eyes. "A siren is connected to the water and draws their power from it. Try to open your mind and feelings to the lake."

Open my feelings to a lake? I closed my eyes and took deep breaths. My mind went blank and my heart seemed to slow. It felt like an eternity went by, waiting for something to happen. I was about to give up when a slight heaviness in my chest made me still. It was a different feeling of when I am in the water. Instead of panic I felt peace and familiarity. My arms felt like they were underwater, and my heart seemed to beat along with the water washing on to the shore.

"I can tell you feel it now. You will have to get used to calling that feeling in order to summon your gifts," Laneli explained.

I opened my eyes and smiled at my tutor, pleased that I was able to connect to the lake in such a short amount of time. "What kind of gifts do sirens have?"

"Their power is mainly in their songs, but siren blessed can slightly control the water as well. We can put just about anyone into a trance by enchanting them. However, we cannot do it to another siren, it doesn't work." She sounded disappointed, as if she had tried it. She studied me for a moment then slowly smiled, having come to a decision. "Let me show you the power of a song." Laneli smiled wickedly and crooked a finger over her shoulder.

Three people I hadn't noticed before walked out from a set of trees. Two of them were the blonde girls hanging around Laneli at lunch yesterday and the other was a Japanese guy who seemed dazed and unfocused. The girls stopped near Laneli and handed her the guy.

"Snap him out of it," Laneli ordered.

One of the girls, with blonde hair in a braid and blue eyes, sang a small song. The guy that stood in the middle of our circle shook his head, aware of his surroundings again and growled at the girls. A small fire burst out onto the guy's hands but Laneli sang a haunting melody and the fire died out. The blank look returned to his face.

I looked at the guy horrified. "What did you do?" I asked incredulously.

"What we are meant to do. Sirens draw people in by their song, although there are some myth blessed people it does not work on and that gets really annoying." She turned to the fire guy under her spell. "This guy is kitsune blessed, not very strong, so he was easy. Now we can do whatever we want." Laneli looked into the Kitsune blessed eyes. "Walk into the water and don't stop."

"What?" Was she for real?

The guy walked forward with a blank stare. He reached the water and kept walking. He was up to his waist before I finally snapped out of my horror-stricken state and rushed toward him. He was up to his stomach now.

"Make him stop!" I yelled.

Laneli crossed her arms and watched the kitsune blessed walk further. "I am showing you what sirens can do. You are one of us now." He was almost up to his shoulders and would be submerged completely soon.

"I said stop!" I screamed, and a sorrowful melody flew from my lips. I didn't know where it came from, but I dared not stop. The guy froze, in the water up to his neck, and I turned to the girls who did it to him.

They stared at me with blank looks, their smiles completely gone. I waved my hand in front of their faces but got no reaction. Did I just enchant them? I decided to use it to my advantage while I still could.

"Walk away. Go all the way to the third floor of the school and stay there for an hour," I told the other siren blessed girls.

They turned in unison and began the walk to the school. That was strange, especially since I shouldn't be able to enchant the other siren blessed. I decided to come back to that weird moment later.

I turned to the kitsune blessed. "Um, come out of the water!" I shouted to him.

The guy turned and walked slowly out of the water. Once he was out, he stood in front of me, dripping water and waiting for further instructions. I didn't know what to do. Well, I did know what I needed to do but didn't know the song to do it.

"Um, snap out of it." I snapped my fingers in front of his face hoping that would do the trick. "La, la, la, la?" I tried but continued looking into an expressionless face.

The only thing left was to take him to Mr. Drakari and hope he could help me get this guy un-enchanted. However, that meant trekking across the quad in full view of the dorms. If anyone saw us, they would think I enchanted this guy for fun. I didn't want that kind of reputation.

"Sit down," I ordered. We were going to sit by the lake until I connected with my inner power and released him from enchantment.

I sat down next to him and closed my eyes. I breathed deeply, bringing in the lake smell then letting the breath out. Over and over I did it until finally I felt a connection to the water. I kept my eyes shut, letting the light flowy feeling go through my body. My mouth opened of its own accord and let out a beautiful song, this time of happiness and peace. I felt that everything would be right in the world if I sang that song.

A few seconds later, I was knocked backwards, and heat beat against the side of my face. I flung my eyes open to see the drenched kitsune blessed hovering over me angrily with a flame in his hand.

"Where are the others?" He asked, with barely contained rage and a bit of fear. Water droplets fell from his shirt to drip on my face, but I didn't dare move to wipe them away.

"I-I sent them away. They were going to make you go under the water. I stopped them," I rushed to explain, holding my hands up to show I meant no harm.

He stared down at me trying to figure out if I was telling the truth. "How did you send them away?"

My eyes still wide, I explained everything that happened from the moment I saw him heading for the water until now with him threatening me with fire. He looked surprised by my story and the flames died out. He offered me a hand and helped me stand up. I dusted myself off and stepped away from him.

"You shouldn't have been able to enchant the siren blessed," he said, studying me curiously.

I shrugged. I didn't know what to say. I was new to this whole siren thing.

"Well, thank you. I'm Ian." Ian held out his hand, this time in greeting.

I nodded and shook his hand. "I'm Serena." My brows furrowed. "Why do they do that to you guys?" I asked remembering the lunchtime fiasco yesterday because Laneli enchanted someone.

Ian shook his head and looked toward the school angrily as if he could project his thoughts to Laneli. "She mainly targets Elliot and his friends. It is a long-standing feud, one that she instigates. I was waiting for Elliot after class and she snuck up on me. Next thing I knew I was here."

Ian looked down at his wet clothes which began smoking. Literal smoke emanated from him and his clothes began to dry. I stared in awe, although I was a little frightened. I figured he knew what he was doing though. Remembering why he had to dry himself made me turn my thoughts to Laneli.

I felt angry for him and his friends. Laneli was taking these people's free will away. I startled, realizing that is what I did by sending the girls away and enchanting the people at Tang's Karaoke. If I continued using this power, I would be able to take away free will. This wasn't a gift; it was a curse. I started walking back to the quad on a mission to see Mr. Drakari to explain Laneli's behavior today. I was not going to stand by and let her bully people.

"Where are you going?" Ian called after me.

“I’m going to Drakari’s office,” I called over my shoulder. “She shouldn’t be able to get away with that. I’m glad you’re okay!”

I left Ian by the lake and marched across the quad, into the school, and to Mr. Drakari’s office. I heard voices inside, but I didn’t care. I was too angry. I burst into the office interrupting the conversation. Dominic Drakari looked up from his desk, surprised by my entrance.

“Ah, we were just about to call you,” Drakari exclaimed, pleased once he got over his shock.

I stopped in my tracks, almost forgetting why I came here. “You were? Why?”

The other person in the room, who I couldn’t see before because of the long back chair they were in, stood up and turned to me. I stared at familiar dark curly hair tied back, bangs hanging down just above her eyebrows, and hazel-gray eyes that almost looked purple.

“Tamara? What are you doing here?” I asked, both confused and excited.

Chapter 5

Best Friend Said What?

"Surprise!" Tam shouted nervously with raised hands.

"What are you doing here?" I asked again and rushed forward to give her a hug.

Returning my hug, she said, "I wanted to see how your first day went."

I stepped back as a thought occurred to me. "How did you get on campus?" As far as I knew, only myth blessed were allowed to enter.

Mr. Drakari and Tam gave each other a knowing look. "I think we should go somewhere to talk," Tam said, guiding me out of the room.

I thought I would have to be the one leading her around, but she seemed to know where she was going. We went down a few halls until we came to a set of double doors and a sign reading library on the front.

Glancing at me briefly, Tam walked into the library. I was getting more confused by the minute. I didn't even know where the library was, yet she had led me straight to it.

She took me away from the tables in the front, to the back of the library where another set of tables were set out. She chose one and sat down, nodding her head to the other side indicating I should take a seat too.

"How do you know your way around so well?" I asked bewildered. A growing sense of understanding was starting to dawn, but I had not figured it all out yet.

Tam twiddled her thumbs and bit her lip nervously. "I've been keeping a secret."

Was she about to admit to being myth blessed? That would explain many of her actions such as having Drakari's number and entering the Academy. I didn't want to rush her since what she was about to say seemed tough for her to admit so I waited, although my foot tapped impatiently.

Tam started to say something but stopped herself. Then with a determined sigh, she laid her hand flat on the table and looked me in the eyes. "I'm a mythological being."

I titled my head in confusion, reminding myself of a puppy. "What do you mean?"

Tam tapped her purple nails on the table and looked around to make sure no one was listening. She leaned forward and whispered, "I'm a djinn."

My eyes widened at her declaration. I had expected her to admit she was myth blessed, but her actual announcement stunned me.

After her admission, a cork must have been pulled because she started spilling everything about the secret she had been keeping. "Seventeen years ago, my mother became a free djinn and met my dad, then they had me. We all had to hide away for almost eight years of my life so I could control my abilities and learn to blend in with humans."

It was odd to hear her say humans as if she wasn't one. Then again, she truly wasn't one. I knew she was homeschooled at an early age, but I never knew it was because she was a djinn. My best friend was a mythological being!

"At one point I was discovered by Drakari, but he never claimed me as most people would have done. He just asked me to be his eyes and ears in school to make sure no one was in danger by other myths and to report if I find any myth blessed." At that point she looked guiltily to me.

So that was why she had Drakari's number and that was why she called him when I enchanted the people in Tang's Karaoke. Something still perplexed me. "Since you are djinn that means I cannot enchant you right?"

Tamara nodded, "I was not affected by you that night, and good for that otherwise we would be in a totally different situation right now."

I didn't want to know what she meant by different situation. "Does that mean I am not able to enchant mythological beings with my songs?" I asked hopefully. The less wills I could take away the better. I didn't want to always have to be watching my back.

"Mmm, kind of. Djinn are immune to most enchantments, but other weaker beings may still be affected." Tam studied me. "Why, what's wrong?"

I shook my head, the anger from earlier coming back. "My tutor, a siren blessed, has no qualms about enchanting innocents and making them do dangerous things." My voice quieted to a whisper and I looked down, focusing on the circles I was tracing with my finger. "I don't want to have that kind of power."

Tam reached out a hand and laid it on mine comfortingly. "You don't have to be that kind of person. You can use your gifts responsibly."

I shrugged not wanting to discuss it more. Tam picked up on my mood and changed the subject. "Tell me about your first day of classes."

I looked up thanking her silently for not pushing the topic of using my gifts. We sat there for a while as we went over the day's events and her life as a djinn over the years. She mentioned how Rae was freaking out about her friend being myth blessed. Apparently, Tam hadn't revealed her secret to Rae otherwise Rae would have something else to freak out about.

It was nice to be with my friend and be part of some kind of normalcy even though our lives were far from normal. I looked at my panda watch and exclaimed, "It's already five! I haven't eaten yet and I need to talk to Mr. Drakari about getting a new tutor!"

Tam chuckled, standing up. "We should probably head back then."

I nodded and stood to leave. It was weird to look at Tam knowing she was not human. Human or not though, it didn't change the fact that she was my best friend.

We walked back to Drakari's office where she checked in with him and waved farewell to us. I waited for her to leave before turning to the principal with a serious expression. "I came here earlier for a purpose, although seeing Tam was a nice surprise."

"She told you everything?" Drakari asked with raised brows.

I nodded.

"Must be different knowing your friend is a mythological being." Drakari watched me carefully. I knew he was waiting to see my reaction.

"It was a shock to find out she is a djinn, but our friendship is no different." We had been friends for way too long to let a simple thing like being a secret powerful mythological being come between us.

Drakari nodded seeming pleased. "What did you need to talk to me about?"

I walked over to the high back chair in front of his desk and sat down, ready to talk. "I need a new tutor. I can't work with someone who is so willing to put people in danger and take their will. If that is what being a siren is then I don't want any part of it. I refuse to use my siren powers."

Drakari held his hands up to slow me down. "Whoa, wait a minute. Tell me what happened."

I explained to him everything that occurred from the moment I saw Laneli by the lake to storming his office after breaking Ian's trance.

Drakari sat back and shook his head looking annoyed. "How many times do I have to talk to that girl?" he mumbled to himself. "I will have to put a guard on her from now on. One that cannot be enchanted." He seemed to remember I was still there and looked at me with sincere and apologizing green eyes. "I will set up a new tutor for you. You will meet at the same place."

Drakari stood up and walked to the door, holding it open for me and effectively ending our conversation.

Before I walked out, he said, "Don't give up on your gifts. There is a lot of good you can do."

I pursed my lips and nodded, not seeing the point in arguing but silently disagreeing with him. He closed the door softly behind me. Laneli seemed like she would be a problem and I was not willing to involve myself with her or that feud she started.

I was not hungry anymore, so I decided to skip dinner. I walked back across the quad toward the water wing, thoughts of my djinn friend and new tutor racing through my head.

"Watch out!"

I looked up at the shout and saw a frisbee flying toward my head. I immediately ducked then stood up straight again when it landed on the grass nearby. I looked around for the owner of the object and saw Ian and Elliot crossing the quad to me.

"Ah, my savior!" Ian shouted with widespread arms.

I put a hand on my hip and raised my eyebrow. "You almost hit me."

"Right, sorry about that," Ian said sheepishly.

We shared a playful smile. It was nice to have another friend even though it was because we both had a problem with Laneli.

"Why did you call her your savior?" Elliot asked, looking between the two of us.

Ian looked guilty again. "Right, um, I didn't want to tell you but Laneli enchanted me."

Elliot looked to have fire in his eyes, and he balled his hands angrily, looking to the water wing as if already thinking of his revenge. Black scales erupted over his skin, but no fire appeared. "When was this?" He growled at Ian.

Ian tapped his chin in thought and looked at me for confirmation as he answered, “About an hour after lunch.”

I nodded in agreement. Ian looked much happier now that he was dry and free. He even reminded me of a playful fox in a way.

Elliot looked upon me with hatred and disgust. I took a step back at the force of it and hurt pinched me. This was the look I was wanting to avoid. This is what being a siren caused. I shook my head and walked toward my dorm. I didn’t need to stand there and be judged for something I didn’t do. There was also no point in arguing. Elliot hated the water myths according to Marion, especially sirens.

“Dude, no need to hate on her. She saved me from them,” I heard Ian say.

I didn’t stop to hear the rest of the conversation. I stomped up the stairs to my room and flung the door open. Marion wasn’t there so I collapsed on my bed and laid there, simmering with annoyance at Elliot and anger at Laneli until I finally fell asleep. I only had to be there for one year, then I would fulfill my plans by moving across the country.

Chapter 6

I'm Seeing Triple

Three days passed since the lake incident, my first day of classes, and since I found out about my djinn best friend. Laneli had made it her mission to bother me at any opportunity by sneering at me, snickering loudly when I walked by, or whispering about me behind my back since I enchanted her and her friends. She never did anything to provoke me into singing, most likely scared of what I could do to her, but it was still annoying. My new tutor became Marion who was helping me find a connection to the water and manipulate it but so far, no luck. She explained to me about natural opposites and weaknesses which I found intriguing. Earth and air are opposites, but spirit did not really have an opposite which made it one of the strongest elements in mythology. Fire and water are natural opposites and they made each other weak which is why fire myths do not often go swimming and water myths do not like fire. It was odd that water myths gained strength in the water, yet my chest tightened with fear and panic every time I was near lakes or the ocean.

Through our training, I could only connect enough to the nearby water to access my siren gifts, but I still refused to use them. Marion and Mr. Drakari tried talking to me about how using my siren abilities could be good, but I didn't know how taking away will was good.

Elliot tried to approach me during gym, but I avoided him, not wanting to see the mistrust and disgust from him. Other than the fact that the school was for students blessed by mythological beings, school was normal.

Thankfully, it was the weekend so there were no classes. Marion explained that every weekend groups of Myth Blessed students would go to town to get away from school for a while. I asked to tag along with her and Devon for a day, feeling like a day out was exactly what I needed. Marion jumped up and down, excited to show me around town.

It was a little after lunch when we decided to go. I put on some sneakers, my panda watch and grabbed my wallet. I left my chestnut hair down to blow in the wind. Marion decided to do a little extra dressing up by adding tinsel to her pigtails and glitter to her face. She said it made her feel magical. She was officially the most interesting roommate.

Marion texted Devon to meet us outside as we walked out of our dorm room. I wasn't looking forward, so I didn't see the solid chest in front of me until I ran into it.

"Oof," I grunted.

Marion plowed into my back and we both stumbled.

"You've really got to stop doing that," the owner of the solid chest joked.

I glared at Elliot "I wouldn't keep doing that if you weren't standing in a path frequently walked."

Marion peered over my shoulder her eyes widening. "What are you doing here?"

Elliot held out a letter with the school stamp on it. "Serena is being summoned."

Marion snatched it from his hands and studied it. "Serena got a summons? That's so cool! When is it?"

"What is a summons?" I asked, taking the letter from Marion and opening it to read.

"Sometimes Mr. Drakari asks students to go on missions. Looks like he is asking you," Marion answered.

I looked at Elliot who nodded in confirmation then read the letter which stated almost the same thing Marion had explained.

Your presence is required at 2:00pm in front of the school on the day this letter is received. You will be going off school property for a classified mission. Your parents have already been notified and give permission.

I checked my panda watch and realized it was almost two. Wow, they don't like giving much notice. I sighed feeling disappointed that I could not go with Marion and Devon to town.

Understanding my sigh, Marion patted me on the back and squeezed passed us. "I guess I will see you later." Marion gave me a small wave and stared at Elliot curiously before walking down the stairs to go to town.

I waved the letter at Elliot. "Lead the way."

We walked down the stairs and left the dorms, walking silently across the quad toward the edge of the school. I wasn't expecting to make any conversation with Elliot, so his voice surprised me.

"I've been wanting to say thank you for what you did for Ian."

I looked sharply at him with suspicion, but he looked back with sincerity and not an ounce of disgust. "Why didn't you say anything before now if you have been wanting to?" I asked.

Elliot's features turned to frustration. "I have been trying to, but you keep avoiding me in gym and I never see you around school. The only reason I was able to get inside your dorm was because I was delivering the summons."

My cheeks reddened with guilt and embarrassment of my behavior but c'mon no one could blame me for wanting to avoid him. He was like the King of Drama at that school. However, I was starting to think his feud was just with Laneli, not all the water myths.

I decided to change the subject. "So, no giant lizard today?"

Elliot chuckled, "He's a Komodo dragon, and his name is Moto."

Komodo dragon, I heard those were dangerous. How did Elliot come to have one as his familiar? "Fine. So, no Moto today?"

"Nah, he will not be able to fit in the car," Elliot answered.

We fell back into silence, not really knowing what else to say as we walked the rest of the way to the front of the school where three people and a black SUV waited.

I blinked in surprise. "Harvey?" Harvey was still in complete black, but his shadows were not as prominent.

When we were close enough, Harvey stepped forward and lifted my hand, putting a soft kiss on top. "Nice to see you, Serena."

My eyes widened and my breath faltered. We stared at each other until a loud snort sounded to our right. I looked toward the sound to see Laneli rolling her eyes at our interaction. She was going with us on this mission? I struggled to hold back an annoyed sigh.

Mr. Drakari cleared his throat drawing our attention to him. Mr. Drakari wore an olive turtleneck and must have shaven his stubbly beard recently, making him look younger. "Alright, let's go. I will explain what our mission is on the way." Drakari looked around to see if we were being watched. "You are not to say anything to anyone about this until it is over, is that clear?"

His words were directed at everyone, but his eyes seemed to linger on me. I nodded but felt even more confused than before. What was this mission and why was it hush hush?

Drakari went around the car to the driver's side while Laneli took the passenger seat. That left Elliot, Harvey and I to take the back. Since I was the smallest of us three, I was positioned in the middle much to my dismay. As Drakari drove the vehicle out of the state park and through town I could see students walking into shops and hanging out making me feel bummed that I couldn't join Marion.

Once we passed town and there wasn't much to look at outside, Drakari told us about the mission. "We have a report about a gorgon blessed turning people to stone. We are going to go help her control her ability then invite her to the school. Our main goal is to isolate her so we can talk. Since she is gorgon blessed and doesn't know how to use her powers, we may need to enchant her to get her away from any people. That is where Laneli comes in. Serena, you will have a chance to see how Laneli uses her gifts in the correct practice," he said, emphasizing correct practice and looking pointedly at Laneli.

I knew why I was invited now. This was Drakari's ploy to get me to use my gifts again or at least see that there was nothing to be afraid of so that I might use them again. Well, joke is on him because this mission will not change anything.

Drakari continued, not hearing my silent promise. "Elliot we will need your strength and immunity if it gets out of hand."

Immunity? Did that mean Elliot couldn't be turned to stone? I realized Drakari did not give Harvey a task. "What are you going to do Harvey?" I asked him.

Harvey glanced at Drakari and Laneli before answering my question. "I'm here to watch over Laneli."

"Watch over her?" I asked crinkling my brows.

"He stalks me," Laneli threw over her shoulder.

Harvey's cheeks reddened. "I'm only doing what I've been asked to do," he told her then turned to me and whispered, "Drakari wants me to make sure she doesn't enchant people anytime she pleases."

I looked at Drakari meeting his eyes in the rear-view mirror. I was glad he followed through and asked someone to watch her. That meant Harvey couldn't be enchanted. He was either very powerful or his myth had immunity. I didn't get a chance to ask what myth he was blessed by because Drakari pulled over and announced that we were at our destination.

I got out of the car after Elliot and looked around at the area around us. It was a tiny town, one that could be driven through in a minute, with farms all around.

"Where can we find her?" Elliot asked, getting right to business.

"She was last seen in town, but our contact says she fled the scene," Drakari answered.

"What does that mean? What scene did she flee?" I asked. They made her sound like a criminal.

Drakari hesitated but must have decided there was no use keeping quiet about the situation. "She turned five people to stone in a grocery store."

Elliot and I gasped. "Can they be changed back?" I asked.

Drakari sighed and the look in his eyes suggested he was unsure. "We have never had a gorgon blessed at our school, but we hope the effects are reversable. I think only a gorgon myth or blessed can reverse it, though."

He hoped? Well that sounded not at all promising.

Drakari turned his attention to Harvey. "Do you think you can check the surrounding areas for a scared girl?"

Harvey nodded, stepping backward into the shade of the SUV and disappeared. I looked expectantly at the other three wondering what we were going to do while he searched but it looked like the plan was to wait for Harvey to get back. I tapped my fingers impatiently against my leg. What would being turned to stone feel like? Would I still be able to see and hear everything? Would it be like I was being smothered? I shuddered thinking about being trapped in stone, silently screaming but not able to be heard.

Harvey reappeared in the shadow of the car. “She is on a farm not too far from here.”

We hopped back in the car and followed Harvey’s directions to a nearby farm on the outskirts of the tiny town. Drakari raced down dirt roads and took turns fast making me slide into Harvey and Elliot. Each time I apologized only to end up crashing into them again. Finally, Harvey called for us to stop and we skidded to a halt in front of a quaint farmhouse.

“Do not look her in the eyes, spread out. Serena stay back but keep an eye out. I will talk to her but if that doesn’t work Laneli you will be up,” Drakari ordered.

We nodded, understanding our orders. I followed them to the back where cows, goats, and chickens wandered around behind fences. Harvey pointed silently to a shed indicating she was hiding in there.

Elliot walked to stand near the shed, Laneli walked to the other side hiding in the shadows with Harvey leaving Drakari in the open facing the door and me a few steps behind.

“Angela!” Drakari called out.

I was surprised to hear the girl's name. I didn't know he knew it, but it made sense. His contact probably told him. I waited anxiously for the door to the shed to open.

"We don't want to hurt you. We are here to help you control your gift. I'm Dominic Drakari, Principal of Myth Blessed Academy!"

We waited in silence, trying to listen for sounds of movement. The shed door creaked open and Drakari called to us, "Keep your eyes averted."

I looked at the ground near the shed door as a girl in red sneakers stepped out. I resisted the urge to look up at her face, instead focusing on her shoes and capri pants.

"You don't need to be afraid," Drakari consoled.

"Th-th-those p-people," Angela sniffed.

I nearly looked up at her, shocked by how young her voice sounded.

"Yes, we know. But they are going to be fine. Where is your mom and dad? Can you come with us?" Drakari took a step toward the girl.

"I-I don't know. My-my sisters." Angela backed up toward the shed.

"We know how scary these new gifts can be. Your sisters will be fine, but we need to get you back to the grocery store so you can reverse the effects," Drakari explained.

A pressure against my leg made me look down. A baby goat was butting its head up against my leg and staring up at me. I shooed it away and focused back on Angela's shoes.

"No, my sisters have to come with us," Angela argued.

"Ok, ok, we can bring you all to town." Drakari reached into his pocket and pulled out a pair of sunglasses. "Can you put these on?"

I could tell Angela hesitated before walking over and grabbing the sunglasses. "Ok they're on."

Elliot, Harvey and Laneli approached us. I finally looked up to Angela's face now that she had the sunglasses on that blocked us from her gaze. Oh, my goodness! She was so young! Probably ten or eleven years old. She had long black hair and freckles. I couldn't imagine being a normal kid one day then turning people to stone the next. Then again, maybe I could understand.

"Do you have two more?" Angela asked nervously.

"Two more?" Elliot asked.

Angela reached out a hand and shouted behind us, "No, they want to help!"

We all turned to see two faces identical to Angela's, however, unlike Angela's we could see their yellow eyes. I heard crackling as if something moved along a stone path. I turned to the noise on my right and covered my mouth with my hand to stifle a scream.

Standing beside me was a stone statue of Drakari. I turned to ask for help but Laneli and Harvey were stone too. The only one left, sporting an identical shocked and panicked look to mine, was Elliot.

I looked down and patted myself checking for stone, but I was normal. How did Laneli turn to stone but I didn't? That same pressure on my leg returned and I looked down to find the same baby goat butting up against me. I shooed it away again as Elliot came to stand beside me.

"Triplets," Elliot groaned. "We should have guessed."

"Why?" I asked, verging on panic.

"Well, gorgons came in threes. So, triplet gorgon blessed makes sense." Elliot stared down the two Angela replicas. "We are not the enemy," he told them slowly.

Angela rushed to her sisters. "Annie, Amber! They are from Myth Blessed. They were trying to help us."

I was afraid to look at their faces but if I was not already turned to stone then I was probably fine. I risked a glance and saw their creepy yellow eyes again, but I held their gaze. "She's right. We think we have a way for you to reverse it then we can take you to the school to learn how to control your ability," I explained.

Annie and Amber looked guiltily at the statues of my colleagues. "How?" they asked in unison.

"Well…" I looked up at Elliot, hoping he would know what to do.

I had never seen him look so helpless. Usually he carried a confident air around him, and I could tell he was trying but he truly did not know what to do. Maybe I could walk them through accessing their gifts like I was taught to do.

"What element are gorgons?" I whispered to Elliot.

Elliot looked at me like I was an idiot. Good to know he can still sport that look no problem. "Earth."

Right, I had that look coming. Stone equals earth. "Girls, I want to try something. Close your eyes." I couldn't tell if Angela did it but the other two did. "Now feel the earth beneath you."

"What?" Annie asked bewildered. "What does that have to do with turning your friends back to human?"

"Just trust me." I waited for them to settle down. "Feel the earth beneath you. Let your minds relax and open up to its solidness and rumbling." I looked at Elliot and shrugged. I didn't know what else to say. Water was easy, it flowed and trickled and crashed against the shore. What did earth do?

Amber stomped her foot and opened her eyes, piercing us with her gorgon eyes. "I can't do it!"

"Sing to them," Elliot suggested.

My head shook with force. I was not doing that.

"You have to, it's the only way right now." Elliot laid a hand on my arm. "You are not Laneli. You can use your song to help."

I glanced at the statues then the frightened girls. "Only with their permission and only this once."

Elliot gave me an appraising look then a slow approving smile formed. Goodness, if I was not preoccupied with this situation, I would review that smile over and over in my mind. His smile was just as good as Harvey's, making him look super attractive and making my heart flutter. I shook my head to clear my thoughts. This was no time for admiring smiles.

I walked over to the girls and knelt. "My name is Serena and I am siren blessed. Do you know what that means?" They shook their heads. "It means that when I sing, I can enchant someone, almost like hypnotize them." Their eyes widened and they looked almost frightened. I didn't blame them. I was the one who was siren blessed and I was still scared. I took a deep breath and continued. "I was wondering if I could sing to you and help you turn them back to regular people."

I waited anxiously for their response. They huddled together, whispering then turned back to me. "We are okay with it. Anything to help them," Annie answered, holding her sister's hands.

I nodded and closed my eyes. It was easy to tap into the water energy inside of me since Marion had been helping. Now I just had to use it to sing, something I had been avoiding all week. This was a crazy twist of fate. I had never really been good at singing, yet now my singing enchanted people.

I opened my mouth and let the melody flow out. The song almost had a mind of its own, already knowing what to do as I knelt there without any idea. I felt the song wrap around the three girl's minds and surprisingly one other mind. When I knew I had hold of them I stopped singing and opened my eyes.

The girls stared blankly ahead. I waved my hand in front of their faces but got no reaction. I turned to Elliot to tell him it worked but froze. He had the same blank look on his face. How was that possible? I thought he was immune. I would have time to worry about it later.

I faced the girls and cracked my knuckles. Here goes nothing. "Can you change them back please?" The girls continued staring straight ahead. I remembered back at the lake when I enchanted Laneli and told her to walk away from Ian. Maybe I had to make it an order. Straightening my back, I ordered, "Change them back to human."

Suddenly the girls' eyes glowed a bright yellow and they stared intently at the statues. Stone slowly cracked and crumbled from the bodies until it was a pile at their feet. Dust coated their clothes but otherwise they were back to normal. I quickly turned to the girls again and ordered them to close their eyes. They did as I told.

"What happened? Harvey asked, groaning. "My body feels stiff."

"Triplets. I should have known," Drakari said, mimicking Elliot's earlier words. He looked around, bending his back to pop it. "What happened to Elliot?"

Drakari waved his hand in front of his face then looked at me with awe. "Did you do this?"

I looked at the ground, my cheeks heating in embarrassment. "I'm sorry. I was only trying to sing to the girls to help you. I don't know how he got that way. Isn't he supposed to be immune?" I babbled. A pressure at my leg made me look down and I was annoyed to see the same baby goat from before. Didn't it know when there was danger nearby? "I thought I told you to go away, you stupid goat."

Baa it bleated at me.

Drakari looked from me to the goat to Elliot, and back at me. "Serena Carter, I think there is more to you than meets the eye," he said intrigued, studying me.

"What do you mean?" I asked, suspicious of his ominous words.

He only shook his head and smiled, "I guess we will find out. Now let's get these girls to the town. Until they undo their work there, we are going to have to leave them and Elliot enchanted."

I finally looked at Laneli, wondering what she thought of my using the siren gift. Her mouth was agape, and she looked at me warily. What was she thinking? Was she mad I used my gift instead of her or was she impressed that I enchanted her enemy? She didn't give me any hint. She walked by and hopped into the car, looking down at her dusty clothes annoyed.

"Harvey can you transport them to town, we will be right there," Drakari asked, turning to the dark clothed man, though it sounded more like an order.

Harvey nodded and rested a hand on one of the girl's shoulders then disappeared in the shade of a tree. I started to follow Laneli to the car but Drakari stopped me. "You are going to have to call him over." Drakari pointed to Elliot.

Right, I should have known that. "Um, get in the car," I called out to Elliot.

Elliot walked robotically to the car and hopped in, continuing to stare straight ahead. I started to follow him, but a loud baa stopped me. I looked behind me at the black and white baby goat that was following me to the car.

"Shoo, go away, you can't come with us" I waved my hands at it, wishing it would leave me alone.

Baa it ran up to me and stood by my side.

"Hmm, very interesting," Drakari said, watching my interaction with the baby goat and rubbing his chin.

"What is so interesting about this?" I asked annoyed with his cryptic words. "Let's just go." I ran to the car and jumped in, closing the door so the goat couldn't follow. Drakari gave the goat one last look before getting into the driver's seat and taking us to town.

Chapter 7

Goat Trouble

We arrived in town shortly after leaving the farm and parked in front of the grocery store that had yellow caution tape preventing anyone from entering. We left Elliot in the car and I made sure that some windows were rolled down for him. I wondered if he would be upset about being enchanted. We approached the store with Drakari taking the lead, but an officer held out a hand to stop us from going any further.

Mr. Drakari held up a badge. “They’re with me,” he told the cop and pointed to us.

The officer waved us through after examining the badge. Being the principal of Myth Blessed Academy must have its perks. The inside of the store was eerily quiet. There were officers standing guard in the corners of the store but otherwise it was only four statues standing in line to check out and a statue clerk at the register.

"We're here," Harvey said from the shadows.

I jumped and spun around. Annie, Amber, and Angela, their eyes still closed, walked out from the shadows with Harvey. Harvey smirked at my reaction and came to stand by me and Laneli.

"Ok, Serena, do your thing," Drakari encouraged, waving his hand toward the statues.

I faced the gorgon blessed triplets. "Turn these people back to human."

The girls opened their eyes and turned their blank stares on the statues. Their eyes flared yellow and a stone cracking noise sounded from the statues. Like before, stone crumbled around them and dust coated their clothes and hair.

"Ok close your eyes." The girls did as I told them once the people were human again.

Drakari walked over to a stand of sunglasses, grabbing two at random and bringing them over to the triplets. He placed a pair over Annie and Amber's eyes then turned to me. "I will pay for those before we leave, but now you can snap them out of the trance."

Relief washed through me. Even though I had the girls' permission, I still felt weird about controlling them. I closed my eyes and reached down into the water energy and sang a melody that felt right. When I opened my eyes, the girls were racing to a woman in line and hugging her dust coated body. The woman the triplets hugged held her hands up away from the girls, looking scared.

"Mommy?" One of the triplets asked, realizing her mother wasn't hugging them back.

"Um, I-" The woman started.

Drakari stepped forward and held out a hand. "Dominic Drakari, Principal of Myth Blessed Academy of Colorado. Can we talk?"

The woman looked relieved and shook his hand. She followed Drakari out of the store, making sure to avoid her daughter's gazes. Her children shuffled behind her, one of them sniffling and another comforting her sister.

"Now what?" I asked Laneli and Harvey.

Laneli rolled her eyes and walked out of the store with her arms crossed, ignoring me. I looked to Harvey who nodded his head toward the doors. We exited the store, leaving the officers to deal with the people who were now back to human. Laneli was standing by the car trying to get the dust out of her hair so we went to stand by her and waited for Drakari.

Suddenly I remembered Elliot. I quickly opened the car door and peered in to see him with a blank face. Aw man, I must sing again. I hopped in beside him and stared at his blank face for a moment. Even enchanted, he looked handsome, but his emotionless face and dead eyes was creepy. I closed my eyes in concentration and sang a soft melody to awaken him. Even though, I had only tapped into the siren gift a few times, it was getting unnervingly easy to use.

A tight grip on my arm made me fling my eyes open. I looked into confused and angry copper eyes. I sighed in relief despite the tight grip he had on my arm.

Elliot let go of me and rubbed his temples. “What happened?”

“Um, well, I sorta accidentally enchanted you.” I braced for his reaction knowing he hated the idea of being under someone else’s control. Especially since his friends kept finding themselves enchanted when Laneli was around.

Eliot pursed his lips and frowned. “I didn’t know that was possible.”

I jumped, startled by this news. Something Drakari said on the way here came back to me. He said Elliot had immunity and I remembered that the gorgon blessed triplets had no effect on him. Yet, I had enchanted him.

Elliot touched my shoulder comfortingly. “Don’t feel guilty. I understand that it was an accident.”

I was surprised by his forgiveness. After everything I had heard about him and his feud with water myths and Laneli, I never would have thought he would forgive something like that. Even when Ian explained what I did to help him, Elliot had exploded in anger. This new, understanding and calm Elliot was weird but nice. I nodded and gave him a small smile.

An annoying baa sounded from outside the car. I froze and shook my head thinking I must be hearing things.

The door beside me opened and an amused Harvey peered in. "There is a goat here."

"What!" I shouted and pushed Harvey aside so I could get a good look at the goat. A white furry baby goat with black patches bleated at me. "That goat keeps following me!"

I heard deep chuckling behind me and turned to glare at Elliot.

Harvey stared at it curiously. "You know, I've only seen this kind of behavior when an animal is a-"

"-familiar." Someone from beyond my line of sight finished Harvey's sentence. Mr. Drakari's face popped into view revealing the owner of the voice. "Serena, I think this little gal is your familiar, although I don't know why your familiar is a goat."

"A goat!" I spluttered. "I don't want a goat. Tell it to go home," I told no one in particular.

"Sorry, Serena but a familiar won't go away. After the power you expressed today, you will need her," Elliot explained with barely contained laughter.

The passenger side door opened and Laneli got in. "I would say I was jealous that you got a familiar before I did, but," she glanced back over the seat with a curled lip at the goat that was trying to jump into the car, "you got a goat, so I think I will be fine."

Baa the baby goat replied.

"Do I have to keep her? Couldn't I get, like, a cat or something?" I asked Drakari pleadingly.

"That's not how it works. A familiar chooses you and it bonds to you. Don't worry, you will come to find that she is a part of you," Drakari explained.

I rolled my eyes, and picked up the goat, bringing it into the car with me. "Great. I have a goat as a part of me."

Drakari looked startled by what I said. He started muttering to himself as he closed my door and walked around to the driver's side. I gave Elliot a confused look who shared my expression and glanced at Mr. Drakari.

The principal didn't explain his reaction and I didn't feel like pushing it. Once Harvey was in the car, we headed back to the school. Apparently, an agent was on scene with the triplets who would finalize their enrollment, so we didn't need to be there anymore. It was crazy how young kids could be when their gifts developed. Those girls' lives would never be the same after the day's events. At least they had each other.

The baby goat slept on my lap and I found myself running my hand along its soft coat. It was an adorably cute baby, but I didn't feel like she would be a good pet to have at a school. I wondered what Marion would think about having to share the room with her.

"What are you going to name her?" Harvey asked from my left.

I stared down at the soft, sleeping goat on my lap, and titled my head in consideration. “Hmm, I don’t know.”

“What about Panda,” Elliot suggested pointing to my watch that was shaped like a panda.

I gave Elliot an amused grin. “You think Panda would be a good name for a goat?”

His cheeks reddened, “I don’t know, I assume you like pandas, so I thought…” he trailed off and shook his head. “Never mind, it’s a stupid idea.”

I looked down at the baby goat, with black patches of fur on its body, and smiled at Elliot. “Panda is a good name.” Elliot and I stared at each other, my cheeks warming at how his copper eyes stared into mine and seemed to heat me up from the inside. Our moment was interrupted by a groan in the front seat.

“You did not just name your goat, Panda,” Laneli said judgingly.

“Oh, stop it Laneli. Panda is a fitting name,” Harvey muttered.

I gave him a thankful smile and decided to ignore her judgement. Three against one for Panda so Panda it is.

We arrived at school not long after leaving the farm area. The streets of the town near the school were still busy with students and I hoped I could still go out sometime to enjoy my weekend. As soon as the car stopped in front of the school, Laneli got out and stalked away.

Harvey rolled his eyes, "I guess I better get to my…stalking."

Harvey opened the door and started to get out but Drakari called out, stopping him, "Harvey, wait." Harvey peered into the vehicle waiting for Drakari to continue. "I was thinking you could take the rest of the day off. I can place someone else on guard for now. Go out and relax."

Harvey gave him a small smile. "Thanks."

Wow, man of few words. We got out of the car letting Drakari go park it. We stood around awkwardly, not knowing what to do now.

"Well, I guess I will see you around." Harvey waved awkwardly.

"Wait!" I stopped him. "Why don't the three of us go out with Marion and Devon to get dinner?" I offered.

Elliot and Harvey glanced at each other. I assume they were trying to figure out if they wanted to hang out with me and each other. I felt like this mission brought us closer, and maybe we could consider each other friends. I just didn't want the day to end.

Baa Panda bleated and bumped into Elliot's leg.

Elliot smiled down at the baby she goat and reached down to pet her. "Alright, I guess I will go." He looked back up to me, "make sure you leave her in your room or the stables. I will be here at seven."

Harvey jumped in. "I will meet you two here as well." I couldn't tell if he was joining because he wanted to or because he didn't want to be left out.

Grinning at them, I jumped up and down a couple of times which I often did when I was excited. When I realized what I was doing, I stopped and looked down, my cheeks heating profusely. "See you later. Bye." I quickly turned and started walking away, leaving behind a couple of attractive chuckling guys.

I hoped Marion was in the room so I wouldn't have to track her down. We trekked up the stairs to the third floor and paused outside the door. "Alright, Panda, here is your new home I guess," I told the black and white goat as I opened my door.

A shrieking girl flew at me and squeezed me with a hug. "How did it go!" Marion squealed.

"I brought home a goat," I told her in response.

Marion stepped back, her face morphing into confusion. The slight glitter left on her face from earlier made the confusion look adorable. "What?"

I closed our door and told her everything about the mission including that it had to do with triplets, when I enchanted Elliot, and how I obtained a baby goat. Marion's eyes got wider as the story progressed. Finally, she looked down at Panda and pet her coat.

"Well, welcome to the water wing, Panda. Just don't eat my shoes." Marion looked over at her pile of shoes near the closet then back to the goat.

Baa Panda sounded in return.

I walked over to my bed and flopped down. "Oh, before I forget, if you're up for it, I was thinking we could go to town for dinner. You could bring Devon."

Marion nodded and went to sit on her own bed, pulling out her phone. "That sounds good. I will let him know now."

I bit my lip wondering what Marion would think about the people I invited. One was the King of Drama at the school and seemed to have a short temper and the other had so many rumors flying around that it was hard to tell what was true. "So, I invited a couple people to join us."

Marion looked up from her phone intrigued. "Who?"

I opened my mouth to answer but a purple smoke filled the room. Marion squeaked in surprise and we both stood up to face whatever it was. I grabbed a notebook off my desk and raised it up to smack whatever was invading our room. Marion took off her shoe and looked ready to tackle the being. Just as suddenly, the smoke dispersed leaving a tall, curly haired woman in its place.

"Tamara? How?" I pointed around the room even though the smoke was gone. I dropped my book back on the desk.

"Surprise! Bet you didn't know djinns could do that," Tamara exclaimed, holding her arms out.

"Dj-Djinn?" Marion squeaked still holding her shoe. Tamara was probably the first mythological being that Marion had seen in person.

"Marion, this is my friend Tamara," I introduced.

"Best friend," Tamara corrected.

I rolled my eyes and continued introductions. "Tamara, this is Marion my roommate."

Tam waved in greeting then shrieked when her eyes landed on Panda. "Why do you have a goat in your room!" Tam shouted, taking a step back from the animal.

I crossed my arms and stared at the goat lying on my bed. At least she hadn't tried to eat anything yet. "Apparently, she's my familiar."

"Shut. Up. You have a familiar already?" Tam came to sit on my bed and pet the baby goat. "Why is it a goat though? Do sirens have some connection to goats that I don't know about?"

"Not that I know of." I looked at Marion wondering if she knew something I didn't, but she shook her head.

I sat on the bed with Tam and Panda, telling her about the mission. I knew Mr. Drakari told us not to tell anyone about it but I figured the triplets were coming to the school anyway and telling only my roommate and my best friend wouldn't hurt anything. The mission was an interesting and frightening experience. I faced three gorgon blessed and survived and found out more things about my powers than I ever thought I would. However,

I did not know if these new developments were a good or bad thing.

"Wow, girl. I am almost jealous of your adventure," Tam admitted.

I shook my head. "Nothing to be jealous about, trust me. Anyway, what are you doing here?"

Tam popped up off the bed as if remembering the reason she arrived in a cloud of purple smoke. "It's the end of your first week at Myth Blessed Academy! I wanted to hang out and hear about everything!"

Tam was a great friend, always knowing when Rae or I needed her company. Come to think of it, her knowing was probably a djinn thing. I missed Rae and wished she could be there with us.

"Sounds good, but maybe next time you could use the door." I pointed to our room door hinting that the purple smoke was unnecessary. Marion nodded from her side of the room finally calming down enough to put her shoe back on her foot.

Tam's smile dimmed. "Right, sorry about that."

Marion spoke up for the first time since finding out there was a djinn in our room. "We were going to dinner later. You should come with us."

Tam looked to me to see if that was alright. I frowned and nodded, holding my hands face up with splayed fingers, silently telling her she was ridiculous for even doubting.

We spent the next couple of hours hanging out in the room, Tam and I telling Marion hilarious stories of our past, and the three of us talking about the past week. Marion was used to the school now, having attended since she was thirteen, so it was interesting to hear her compare this year to other ones. When asked about how she met Devon, her cheeks reddened, and her skin turned translucent.

"We were sophomores and at the time I preferred to be around the lake rather than people. Well, one day an eagle flew down to me and perched on my shoulder. I was terrified and dare not move." Marion looked off to the side remembering the moment and smiled. "Devon came running and apologized profusely as he gathered his familiar up. At that time, Devon had only had Gus for a few weeks and was still getting used to his ways. Instead of leaving, he sat down next to me and we talked, and every day since then." Marion looked back at us still blushing. "And that's about it."

"Aww," Tam and I shared.

It was amazing how familiars could be so influential in our lives. I glanced at Panda and sighed. Even though she was a barn animal and it made no sense as to why she was mine, I knew she was important and special. My stomach grumbled reminding me of food.

I glanced at my panda watch and realized it was already 6:45. "Hey, we should go meet the others. Elliot and Harvey said they would be in front at seven."

We grabbed our phones, keys, and wallets then headed out to meet everyone in front of the school. Marion told Devon to meet us there as well. As we were leaving, I looked at sleeping Panda on my bed. I hoped she would stay asleep, otherwise she might freak out and disturb the neighbors.

The boys were standing around awkwardly waiting for us. Their hands were shoved into their pockets and they avoided each other's eyes. Devon and Elliot must have left their familiars behind because they were nowhere to be seen.

Devon looked up, visible relief showing on his face. He rushed forward and gave Marion a kiss. The movement caught Elliot and Harvey's attention, causing them to look up and watch us approach.

"Ooo, who're the hotties?" Tamara whispered to me.

I waved at Elliot and Harvey, feeling heat rush to my cheeks at Tam's words. "This is Elliot and Harvey. You guys, this is my friend Tamara," I introduced loudly, ignoring her hotties comment.

Elliot nodded in greeting keeping his hands in his pockets. Harvey took Tam's hand and raised it to his lips like he did to me the first time we met. Tamara's eyes widened as Harvey placed a kiss on her hand. She glanced at me with her mouth agape, wondering what was happening but I could tell she enjoyed it due to the red in her cheeks.

“Yeah, he does that,” I chuckled. I looked around to see if everyone was good to go. “Ready?” I asked no one in particular.

The group nodded and we headed out to town, taking Devon’s car since his was the biggest. Tamara probably could have poofed us there, but she couldn’t go around revealing her djinn identity. The town looked nice and quaint especially with the hanging lights and old-fashioned lamp posts along the streets.

Marion directed Devon to a pizza parlor not too far from the State Park, where we got a circular corner booth to fit us all. Music played in the background and there were a few other groups there enjoying the pizza and atmosphere. A couple of people gave Elliot wary looks, most likely expecting drama to go down. Other people from Myth Blessed Academy gave our group strange looks, probably wondering what Elliot and Harvey were doing hanging around us.

While we waited for the pizzas to arrive, Tam kept the flow of conversation going when we fell into uncomfortable silence a few times. “So, what myths are you all blessed by?”

Marion answered proudly from the other side of the table, “Water Sprite.”

“Griffin,” Devon added holding a finger in the air.

Harvey was next and I waited eagerly for his answer. I had been wondering all week what myth would have to do with shadows. Harvey looked at the table and picked at the edge, "I'm Nalusa Chito blessed."

"Nalusa Chito?" I asked. I had never heard of that before.

"It's a shadow being from Choctaw mythology. It is known for being a soul eater," Harvey explained. He shook his head and shrugged, "It's a spirit myth."

A soul eater? Could Harvey eat souls? I almost didn't want to know. I think I understood what he meant by shadow being though since he constantly looked like he was wrapped in shadows. I decided to research Nalusa Chito and Choctaw more when I got back to school.

Tam was beside Harvey, but we skipped her, the others assuming she was human, which made me next. "Siren," I shared although everyone at the table already knew my myth.

That left Elliot. I was pretty sure all of us, even Tam, knew about his myth as well but he shared it with us anyway, "Dragon."

At that moment, our pizzas arrived, and we fell into silence. Marion and Devon talked quietly to each other. Harvey looked uncomfortable but Tam didn't seem to notice as she flirted with him. Elliot seemed tense and quiet, so I didn't know whether he was open to conversation or not. Since he was the only other person I could talk to without interrupting another conversation I decided to give it a shot.

"What is your problem with water myths?" I asked wanting to know the history behind the feud. Elliot scowled at his pizza and I waved my hands at him, wanting to reassure him that he didn't have to answer. "You don't have to explain, it's none of my business. Sorry I asked." I took a bite of my pizza, trying to show him it was no big deal.

Elliot sighed, and his scowl was replaced with resignation. "No, I'm sorry. It is well known that water and fire myths don't get along because we are natural opposites. However, my feud is not with all water myths, just Laneli."

I remembered Marion mentioning water and fire were natural opposites and I also figured his feud was with Laneli, but why?

"Her and her friends have no qualms about controlling people with their songs, and one time it got way out of hand. She made my best friend betray me and end up getting expelled. There was no evidence of enchantment, so my friend took the fall. I know it was her though, and I have been fighting her ever since."

Anger rose up inside me. I had only been there a week and already I had seen Laneli's mistreatment of people and power. "Why doesn't she get expelled? I saw what she did to Ian but all they did was put a guard to watch her."

Elliot shook his head, the same anger I was feeling showing on his face. "Her mom works at the school so she gets away with more than she should."

I sat back in shock. Her mom works at the school. Well, that explains why she keeps getting chances to redeem herself. I looked to Elliot and saw sadness under his anger. I laid a hand on his arm causing him to look into my blue eyes and see the sincerity in them.

"Just know that I will never use my siren abilities for personal gain. I'm sorry about your friend."

Elliot nodded. "Thanks. I trust you. Especially after what you did for Ian."

We stared at each other a moment longer, heat seeming to rise between us. A look of confusion and desire shown in his copper eyes and I was sure an answering look shown within my gaze. He leaned forward a little and my breath caught. What was he doing? Was I ready for this? I barely knew him, yet I feel like I have always known him. The sound of metal crashing on the table ruined the moment and I looked over to see Marion looking guiltily at the pizza pan that she bumped. I sat back and nervously bit into my pizza, hoping my cheeks were not flaming.

If there was anything I took away from the night, it was that I knew I should never listen to rumors. That and the fact that I now had a crush on a certain dragon blessed. Rumors twisted the truth and did more harm than good. It was always good to go directly to the person being talked about to find out the truth or ignore the rumor. Now that I understood Elliot more and realized his feud had more meaning than just water versus fire, I wondered what the truth was behind the rumors about Harvey.

Chapter 8

Heating Things Up

I was glad I invited Harvey and Elliot to dinner, and that Tamara could join us. I told her to bring Rae next time so we could have a girl's night out. Panda was not happy when we returned and since that night, she had been determined to follow me wherever I went. For the rest of the weekend, I ended up relaxing and finding out how to feed Panda and how to stop her from following me to the bathroom. Now, the weekend was over, and I was back to having to worry about school.

Myth history was officially my favorite class. I had learned more about different kinds of water mythological beings than ever before. We were still on the water unit and today we finally talked about sirens.

"Sirens in the earliest mythology were depicted as having the body of a bird and the head of a woman. Over time, those depictions changed but usually, the being was always part bird, part woman," Mr. Jamens began. "Some myths describe sirens as half human, half fish, almost like a mermaid. No matter what the physical description was, one thing was always consistent. Sirens had the ability to lure humans to their deaths by enchanting them with their singing."

I received some stares from my peers, but I ignored them. I did not have to follow the siren path of leading people to their deaths. I tried picturing what a bird woman would look like. All I could think about was a chicken with a human head. I looked down to my baby goat lying near my seat. If birds were a big part of sirens, then why was my familiar a goat? The other form of a siren, an enchanting half woman half fish seemed to ring truer in my mind. A flashback to Hawaii came unbidden to mind. I was seventy percent sure I saw a flash of scales when I was being tossed around in the water. However, that still did not explain the goat.

Mr. Jamens continued his lecture by discussing the stories of sirens with Demeter, Odyssey, and the Muses. I took tons of notes and found myself picturing all the stories in my mind. Myth History was the only class that seemed to fly by. The next three classes were slow and boring, but I got through them until finally it was lunch time.

My favorite time.

I was now knowledgeable of the layout of the school, so I was able to make my way to the cafeteria efficiently. Our usual table was empty when I arrived, so I grabbed some food and sat down, feeding pieces of a sandwich to Panda while I waited for Marion and Devon. My phone buzzed as I was searching the room for my friends. I sighed when I saw the message.

Hey, I'm going to eat in the library today. Gotta study! - Marion.

Well, I guess I will eat alone then. I hated eating alone. As if summoned by my thoughts, a tray dropped onto the table next to mine causing me to jump and place a hand over my heart. I looked up to see shoulder length dark hair and dark eyes.

"May I join you?" Harvey asked.

I gestured to the empty table letting him know it was open and he could sit. Harvey sat across from me and pulled his tray closer. He ripped off a piece of tomato from his burger and leaned down under the table to feed it to Panda. I smiled at the sweetness of his action even though Panda didn't need any more food.

We ate in silence for a few minutes and I couldn't tell if it was comfortable or awkward. Harvey picked at his food and fidgeted with the tray. He opened and closed his mouth a couple of times, looking as if he wanted to talk but couldn't find the words.

After the third time of opening and closing his mouth I spoke up to encourage him, "What's on your mind, Harvey?"

"There's something I've been wanting to ask you." He fidgeted with the tray some more, avoiding my eyes.

My heart started racing in dread and anticipation. It sounded as if he was about to ask me out, but I did not want him to. Harvey had been turning out to be quite sweet and not at all scary like the rumors kept saying. He was handsome in a way that I was not used to seeing and seemed to like hanging out with me and my friends. However, I didn't think I would ever want to be more than friends.

"Har-" I started to say in a soft voice to let him down easy, but his next words stopped me.

"I was wondering if your friend has asked about me." Harvey looked nervously at me.

My brows drew together, as I tried to figure out what he was talking about. "My friend?"

Harvey's cheeks reddened leaving a bright splash of color against his dark clothing. "Um, yeah, the one from the other night. Tamara."

A slow smile spread across my face until I was grinning crazily at him. "Oh. My. Gosh. You have a crush on Tam?"

Harvey looked around to see if anyone heard me. "Um, I wouldn't say that. Never mind about it." He grabbed his tray and stood.

I put my hand on top of his to stop him from leaving. "No, no it's okay. I won't tell anyone. I haven't really talked to her since that night." I tried making eye contact, but he avoided my gaze. "I could find out how she feels if you want."

Harvey took a moment to think about it. He sat back down and bit into his burger. I waited patiently for him to give me an answer as I ate. Finally, he met my eyes. "Sure. Just don't tell her what I said. Recon only, ok?"

I mock saluted him. "Yes, sir."

His nervous expression was replaced by a smile at my silliness. I was glad we had something to keep us friends and not make things awkward. We ate the rest of our lunch then dropped off our trays and left the cafeteria together but separated at the end of the hall to go to our classes.

I arrived at gym, receiving the usual judging stare from the coach for arriving one minute before class started. It wasn't my fault that class started exactly five minutes after lunch or that the outside gym area was across campus from the cafeteria. Thankfully, I was never the one to receive the full display of a judging stare and tapping of the watch because Elliot always arrived after me.

Elliot came to stand beside me and this time I didn't move away. Last week, I made it my mission to avoid him and his hatred, but I now knew that he didn't mean to react in an angry way and that his hatred was for Laneli. A hatred that I shared.

"Now that everyone is here," coach started with a pointed stare in our direction, "I want us to begin combat. Anything goes so use your gifts, fighting skills, anything. Today is about assessing where you are and how I can help you throughout the semester."

Excited muttering filled the area though I had no idea what they were excited about. I was terrified. I had no fighting ability unless you counted Mortal Kombat or Super Smash Bros. and I was not going to use my siren ability. That left a nonexistent water affinity I could use so it looked like I was doomed.

"When I call your name, you will move into the circle and begin," coach ordered. "First up, Darsden and Camilla."

Two people stepped forward and faced each other while we stood in a circle around them. Without any warning, Camilla disappeared and a moment later Darsden was tackled to the ground by an invisible force.

"What myth is she?" I whispered, not expecting anyone to answer.

"Sylph," Elliot answered beside me. "An air myth"

I looked up at him, but he had his eyes on the fight. Darsden got up from the ground and in the blink of an eye he was behind Camilla squeezing her. She flickered back into view then jumped in the air, taking both of them many feet off the ground to hover in place. I stared with a slack jaw at the show of elemental power. Darsden looked panicked as his feet dangled. He slipped and caught her waist stopping his fall, but Camilla wrapped a wind tunnel around them trying to knock him off. Darsden opened his mouth and bit her leg. With a pained squeak the wind died and they both fell from the sky, landing hard on the ground. With his super speed, strength, and biting I figured at that point that Darsden was vampire blessed. Darsden got up but Camilla was still knocked out. Coach made a mark in his book then signaled a couple of people to grab Camilla to move her.

"Good show of abilities. Remember people, you can also punch and kick." It was disturbing to see coach enjoy the violence we were inflicting on one another.

A few more fights occurred allowing me to see a wide variety of abilities and myth blessed. I watched as a harpy blessed used her nails to tear through the clothing and skin of a golem blessed. Thankfully, the golem blessed could heal himself with some clay. My ears nearly bled from the scream of a banshee blessed and my heart almost stopped from the howl of an amarok blessed.

"Next up, Elliot and Serena," coach called out.

My heart stuttered. I had to fight Elliot? Big, tough, prone to bursts of fire, dragon blessed Elliot?

I was going to die.

I told Panda to stay by the edge then faced Elliot in the middle of the circle just as all the other people before us did. My palms were sweaty, and my heart raced. Elliot gave me an apologetic look before conjuring a fireball to his hands and making scales break out over most of his skin. It was weird and terrifying to see a lizard man in front of me holding fire. I also saw wariness from him but couldn't tell if he was afraid to attack or was afraid that I would use my siren ability on him. Now that we knew my siren gift would work on him, I didn't blame him for being wary.

I tried to control my breathing and connect to the water energy within me. I felt myself accessing the siren ability, but I forced it down and searched within for an affinity with water. If I could just douse his flames, then I would have a level playing field. Elliot threw a fireball at me breaking my concentration. I ducked down and rolled to the side causing grass and dirt to stain my jeans. I grabbed some dirt and grass from the ground and threw it at Elliot. He easily dodged it, but it gave me enough time to get in close to him and punch him in the face.

I clapped my aching hand over my mouth in shock at what I just did. Elliot frowned at me and rubbed his jaw but didn't seem fazed by my attack. Then he started laughing. I looked at him in confusion then anger when he didn't stop. How could he laugh when I just punched him and got a sprained wrist as a result? That wasn't fair.

I used my other hand to punch him in the belly. I didn't get far because he just grabbed my wrist and yanked me forward. I lost my balance and stumbled into him. He wrapped me in crushing arms that started to heat up with fire. He was going to burn me!

I struggled to get out of his hold, doing everything including stepping on his feet, punching him in the belly, and kicking him in the shins. None of it worked. The heat was going to make me have heat stroke and burns all over my arms if I didn't do something fast. I still refused to use my siren gift, but it was starting to look like that was my only option. The fire was flickering on his arms and hands now and I could smell burning hair. The coach needed to end the fight before I was a charred heap on the ground. The warmth of the fire wrapped around me until I screamed. I screamed so loud that people around us flinched away. I did not scream out of fear or pain though. I screamed out of anger.

I was trapped in dragon blessed arms that were on fire and I felt helpless. I did not want to have to rely on my siren gift to take away Elliot's will. I should be able to take care of myself in a different way. I heard coach telling Elliot to let go of me and the match was over, but it sounded muffled. A roaring sound in my ears caused a migraine and my vision started to go black. My chest burned and felt constricted like it did when I was in the water.

My throat started burning and something was putting immense pressure on my lips from within until I couldn't keep my mouth closed anymore. I felt Elliot release his hold on me and ask if I was okay, but the roaring was louder, and the burning was hotter despite there not being any more fire on his person.

I opened my mouth thinking I was about to puke all over Elliot, which would have ended my life in a completely different way, but fire poured out instead.

That's right. I was breathing freaking fire!

When it was all out of my system, my temperature fell instantly to normal leaving my body to collapse and go into shock. Elliot rushed to my side asking what was happening, but I couldn't hear him. My ears were buzzing, and my vision was fading. The last thing I saw before I passed out was coach and Elliot kneeling beside me with the class in the background trying to see what happened. I'm pretty sure I also saw a giant hole in Elliot's shirt with charred edges.

Chapter 9

Dual Myths

A beeping noise broke through the haze of my mind. I blinked until my eyes adjusted to the light and looked around a clean, sterile room with a heart monitor near my bed. I wasn't one of those clichés in movies that couldn't remember anything after being unconscious. All those memories of burning from the inside out, chest constricting, and breathing fire were unfortunately easy to recall.

"Hello?" I called out.

I was surprised that my voice came out clear rather than scratchy. I would have expected breathing fire to have some kind of negative effect on my throat.

I wanted answers about what I did and if Elliot was alright. I went to sit up but a pain in my hand made me hiss. I looked down to see my right hand wrapped in bandages. I must have hurt myself when I punched Elliot in the face. That's embarrassing.

A middle-aged woman with blonde hair pulled back in a ponytail and crystal blue eyes outlined in heavy mascara moved aside a curtain and appraised me. "Well, well, look who's up. I knew it wouldn't take you long," she said in a cheery voice and pasted on a bright smile outlined in pink lipstick. "I'm Nurse Lydia."

Beyond the curtain I could see more beds that were filled with students. The nurse bustled around the bed with a thermometer to take my temperature.

"I never liked the second week of school. Too many kids coming in here injured from those battles that fool of a coach makes them do. You're lucky you have a high fire tolerance otherwise you'd be in here for a whole lot more than a fever and a bruised wrist." Nurse Lydia held out a device and urged me to put my finger in it. She stared down at the thing until it beeped then wrote the data on a sheet by my bed.

"Fire tolerance?" I asked remembering the lesson about natural opposites in my tutoring with Marion. "How is that possible?"

"Your guess is as good as mine, ducky," the nurse said. "That's why I notified Mr. Drakari as soon as you were brought in. I will call him, so he can head over here now." She shuffled away leaving me to ponder the new knowledge.

A furry animal jumped onto the bed nearly crushing my stomach on its landing. “Aw, Panda you stayed with me.” I pet her on her nose then shifted her, so she was sitting by my side rather than on top of me.

“I heard you were awake,” Elliot said as he walked into my line of sight.

He had a fresh shirt on, and his black hair was just as spiky as usual, but annoyingly he had no bandages. Not that I was wishing him harm or anything. I just felt that since I hurt my hand with his face then he should have a bruise or something from my attacks. Although I am relieved to see that my belching fire had not affected him.

“What are you doing here?” I asked.

Elliot took a seat in a chair by my bed. “Well, sirens don’t usually breathe fire, so I wanted to see if you were ok.”

“I’m fine. I think. I want answers though and Mr. Drakari is on his way to give them to me.” I hesitated before asking him, “Do you want to stay and hear what he has to say?”

Elliot gave me a bright smile that made my heart race. “Of course.” He stretched out an arm and pet Panda on her back.

We didn’t have to wait long before Drakari was rushing over to me. “I heard what happened and well, first off, how are you?” He seemed agitated and excited.

"I'm fine. So, why did I breathe fire?" No sense in beating around the bush. I wanted to get straight to the point.

"Good. I am very intrigued by your predicament, but I think I know why it happened." Drakari started pacing. "You see, I've been wondering why a goat became your familiar."

I titled my head in confusion, wondering where this was going. What did Panda have to do with breathing fire? Elliot seemed just as lost as me.

"I've been searching my books and researching sirens, but I've been researching the wrong myth this whole time!" Drakari turned to us with arms outstretched to the sides of him, grinning like he figured out the answer to the universe.

"I'm lost Mr. Drakari. Why would a siren be the wrong myth?" I asked.

Elliot eyes started widening slowly as he figured out what the Principal was saying and gawked at me. His reaction made chills go down my arms.

"What? What is it?" I asked, getting a little scared by their expressions of awe and curiosity.

"You probably haven't taken the fire unit in myth history yet, but do you know what a chimera is?" Drakari asked steepling his fingers.

I shook my head. I really needed to brush up on mythological beings.

Drakari started pacing again as he explained, "A chimera is a hybrid of a lion, goat, and snake that breathes fire."

I looked to Panda, watching the innocent little goat sleep away as if my whole life didn't change again when she came into my life. "So, are you saying..." I couldn't bring myself to say the words.

Drakari stopped again and faced me. "Based on your display at gym today and your familiar, I am ninety-seven percent sure you are chimera blessed."

"Look at her arms." My head whipped to Elliot at his words. "Her arms aren't singed or burned like they should be. I used fire on her."

Drakari tapped his lips with a finger. "Hmm, yes, it seems as if you have some fire tolerance. In fact, Elliot's fire may have been what triggered the chimera gifts in you."

I shook my head in disbelief and wonder. "I-I am siren and chimera blessed?" I asked slowly. How is that possible?"

"I believe you may have had one of them since you were young and got the other at a later point in your life." Drakari mused. "Do you have any idea which one came first?"

For most of my life I had been normal. Even during my exam to see if I was myth blessed, I was normal. Now I am blessed by two myths. I had no idea when these mythological beings would have blessed me, and I never showed any signs until a week ago. I couldn't even think of anything strange that would have triggered either one.

Wait.

A song was coming to mind from when I was in Hawaii. I almost drowned in the water. In fact, I probably should have died that day. Throughout that experience I kept hearing a haunting, sorrowful song. Before I knew it, I was suddenly on the beach. Then, during my Karaoke incident I heard the same song from Laneli. Could Hawaii have been where I was blessed by a siren?

I looked to Drakari with my head titled, still thinking about the event and if it connected with what was happening now. I told Drakari and Elliot everything about what happened in Hawaii including hearing the song which I had kept quiet about for weeks. Drakari bit his lip and nodded as I spoke.

"Yes, if that is what you experienced then it may have indeed been a siren you saw that day. The whole point of a siren song is to lure people into the water to drown so I do not know why they blessed you instead," Drakari confirmed what I had been thinking, "but whatever the reason, you now have two myth blessings,"

I nodded to show I understood, though Hawaii only explained when and where I was blessed by a siren not a chimera. Panda shifted beside me and I looked down at the sleeping kid. It made so much sense now why a goat was my familiar, but I was still disappointed. The universe could have given me something cool like a lion or a snake instead of a goat.

"I also do not know why your chimera side, which I assume you got first, stayed hidden and dormant for so long." Drakari snapped his fingers. "I will research some more." He started to leave excitedly but stopped and glanced over his shoulder. "Oh, before I forget, Elliot will be your tutor for this new development." Drakari walked away not waiting for a response, muttering, "This is unprecedented. What does this mean? How did it happen?"

When he was gone, I focused my attention on my new tutor. "So, I guess you will be teaching me some fire stuff, huh," I said trying for casual conversation. My fingers twiddled with the blanket I was under as I waited for his response.

Elliot stared at the floor lost in thought with an unreadable expression. He didn't seem to have heard me. Was he angry at this new development? Was he hurting from an injury after all?

"Elliot?" I asked concerned.

He shook his head and looked at me. "Hmm?"

"Are you ok?" I asked instead of repeating my earlier comment.

He slowly nodded. "Yeah. I was just thinking about you being siren and chimera blessed. It…seems like it might become problematic."

“Why?” I titled my head in confusion. It looked like head tilting was becoming too common for me these days. I had to break that habit.

“Well, don’t take this seriously because I don’t actually know anything about your situation, but…” Elliot paused, looking hesitantly at me.

“Oh, just spit it out!” I shouted impatiently causing Panda to lift her head in my direction.

“I was thinking about how water and fire are natural opposites that weaken each other. What if having both affinities causes you problems?”

I frowned, thinking about what he said. According to Drakari’s mutterings when he left, my situation was unprecedented so there was no evidence that fire and water would weaken me. Even if it did weaken me, what was the worst that could happen?

“Maybe it will be balanced,” I suggested.

Elliot shrugged like he wasn’t convinced, but the nurse walked back over to me preventing him from saying anything more.

“Alright, you are all good to go, ducky,” the nurse announced.

I smiled in relief. I did not want to be stuck here any longer. I nudged Panda moving her to the floor and threw back my covers. Elliot stood up and stuck his hands in his pockets.

“Thanks for-” I started to say to the nurse.

“Mom!” A whining female voice interrupted.

The nurse turned around to face the owner of the voice. “What’s wrong, honey?”

“That stupid shadow guy won’t leave me alone!” The girl complained.

I moved to the side so I could see who was in front of the nurse. I gasped when I saw the blonde hair, blue eyes, and scowl of Laneli. The nurse was Laneli’s mother?

Elliot groaned low enough for only me to hear and grabbed my arm, steering me away from the family. We attempted to sidle by unnoticed, but a disgusted snort stopped us.

“If it isn’t dragon boy and goat girl.”

I turned to Laneli. “Seriously? That’s the best you could come up with?”

Laneli curled her lip and bobbed her head mockingly. She looked like she was going to say something else, but her mother stopped her.

“Now, now, honey. Don’t talk to students like that. I will talk to Mr. Drakari about your shadow.”

Laneli rolled her eyes and crossed her arms. Elliot and I didn’t wait for her response. We quickly maneuvered our way past them and left the nurse’s office.

When we were far enough away, I laughed. “Well, I didn’t think I could be shocked anymore today.”

“Yeah, the nurse is why she doesn’t get expelled.” Elliot shook his head in annoyance.

We walked down the halls in comfortable silence until we were out on the quad. This was where we would separate but I couldn't bring myself to walk away from him yet. I was touched that he came to visit me in the nurse's office.

"So, siren and chimera huh?" Elliot asked, kicking at a piece of grass.

"I guess so. Hey, are you ok?" I hadn't seen any damage but maybe it was underneath his shirt.

"What do you mean?" Elliot gave me a curious glance.

"You know, when I, um, breathed fire on you." I bit my lip in embarrassment.

Elliot gave me an amused smile. "Oh, you mean when you vomited fire on me?"

My nose scrunched up in disgust. No one needs that image in their mind. I had a feeling that he wouldn't let me live that down.

Elliot laughed at my reaction. "Yeah, I'm fine. I'm fireproof after all, courtesy of some dragon that decided to bless me in the womb."

I turned to him in astonishment. "Wow! That young? How do you know?"

Elliot gave a small smile and looked off toward our dorms. "It is my mom's favorite memory and she never celebrates a birthday without telling it." He chuckled as he remembered the birthdays. "Anyway, I guess I will see you for tutoring tomorrow afternoon."

“Yes, I will be there.” I waved to Elliot as he split off to head toward the fire wing.

It was interesting and unnerving to realize that I could be part of either wing now. In fact, since I was chimera blessed first, I should technically be in the fire wing rather than the water. I shook my head at the thought. I would never give up being roommates with Marion.

This whole new experience, being blessed by two myths and having dual affinities, was threatening to overwhelm me but I decided to make the best out of it. I could train myself to breathe fire which I found slightly better than singing though it sounded painful. I could work on controlling water and fire and see how the balance of the two worked out. I looked down at Panda trotting beside me. With some answers came more intrigue it seemed.

At least my mother will have something else to celebrate about.

Chapter 10

Water and Fire

When I told Marion and Tamara about my dual myths, they freaked out but surprisingly in a good way. Marion believed it was a breakthrough into why I couldn't manipulate the water. We planned to use that knowledge to better help me connect, which was where we were now. Marion and I sat by the lake the day after the gym incident attempting to connect me to the lake energy. Unfortunately, it was not just Laneli that encouraged meditating.

Panda lounged under a tree close by but far enough away to avoid the water. The little goat was like me in that way. Not wanting to be close to the water but unlike me she had a choice.

"So, what I'm thinking is you should embrace your fire affinity then reach out for the water," Marion directed.

"Mmm, that doesn't seem as easy as you make it out to be. I don't even know how to access fire." My eyes were still closed but I could almost feel Marion's frown.

"Try imagining water flowing through your limbs while heat warms you inside. Let's see what that does," Marion suggested.

I did as she said and pictured water flowing from my shoulders out to my arms and fingertips. The energy came readily enough but it was only enough to use my siren gifts. This time I imagined fire sitting inside my body, warming me from the inside out. The warmth increased until I was sweating yet the water continued to flow through my limbs. Suddenly a searing pain in my head caused me to gasp and double over. My chest started constricting making it hard to breathe. I had only ever felt that kind of pain in the water but this time it was much worse.

Marion scrambled forward and rested her hand on my back. A feeling like a small blanket of energy radiated from her hand filling me with water energy and serenity. The pain started to go away and soon I could only feel the water energy. Once I had my breathing under control, I lifted my head to look at a frightened Marion.

"I don't think that was the right thing to do," I said, my hands shaking on my legs.

Marion pursed her lips and got to her feet, pointing to the middle of the lake. "Maybe the thing we need to do is go out there."

I stood up and backed away from the lake. "Um, I don't think so."

Marion turned to me with a hopeful look. "I think this might work! C'mon let's do it. There is a ca-"

"No!" I shouted. I didn't mean for it to sound so harsh, but my heart raced, and my body wanted me to run far away from the lake. I was acting out of fear. "No," I said softer. "I think I am done for the day. I will see you at dinner."

I left a shocked Marion standing by the lake and walked back toward the quad, calling Panda to follow. I felt terrible for shouting at my friend who was only trying to help me. It was just that the thought of going out into the water terrified me, especially after feeling the pain in my chest. I had been afraid of deep waters for my whole life. My parents told me that when I was younger, I would swim in pools, but I refused to swim in the ocean or lakes.

I would have to apologize to Marion sooner rather than later. Maybe with chocolate cake. She loved cake.

I wished I could go to my room and hide away for a while until dinner, but I had one more class I needed to go to. That is if fire training counted as a class. I veered left, away from my dorm and headed to an area near the gym. Apparently, that was where fires could be made on school property and be easily contained in case it got out of hand.

I saw Elliot sitting in a lawn chair waiting for me even though I didn't need to be there for another twenty minutes. His black hair looked extra spiky today and he wore a soft gray t-shirt. A giant lizard, Komodo dragon, laid on the ground to his left. Elliot waved his hand at a circle of stones and fire sprang to life in the middle. He waved his hand again making the fire die. He brought the fire back to life with another wave of his hand looking distracted and bored. He was about to wave his hand at the fire once more, but I came up behind him and tapped his shoulder, causing him to jump.

"You're early," Elliot commented but didn't ask why. "Take a seat."

I sat in the chair next to him and guided Panda to sit on the ground on my right, as far away from Moto as possible. I didn't want the giant lizard eating my goat. My body leaned forward, drawn to the heat of the flames that flickered mere inches from us. It felt like a blanket of warmth that seeped into my skin, giving me energy. I closed my eyes, basking in the feeling.

"Wow, you seem to already be able to access the fire energy," Elliot whispered beside me. His breath felt hot against my cheek and my skin tingled at his nearness.

I cracked my eyes open and studied him. "Why do you sound surprised?"

I was surprised as well but I didn't want him to know that. It took almost a whole week for me to access the water energy easily, but all I had to do for fire was sit down and let it wash over me. It was bizarre.

"I'm not used to tutoring someone who already has access to it, that's all." Elliot shifted back into his chair. "I want to see what you can do."

I opened my eyes all the way, eager to learn as long as he didn't ask me to touch the fire. My body stiffened at the thought of having touch it and panic threatened to overwhelm me. I quickly took a deep breath, reminding myself that he hadn't asked me to do anything yet. I failed in water training earlier. I didn't feel like failing in fire, too.

"The simplest task anyone first learns, well, after they learn to access the energy, is to make a fire." Elliot waved his hand at the flames and the fire died down until it was just smoke. His copper eyes twinkled in amusement at his skill. He gave me an encouraging nod toward the middle of the stone circle wanting me to make a fire with my mind.

I looked from him to the smoke in front of us, raising an eyebrow in doubt. I decided to mimic him and waved my hand toward the stone circle. I expected a fire to burst to life, even if it was only a small one, but the only thing I managed to do was disrupt the smoke trail drifting in the air.

"Hmm, try picturing the fire in your mind and remember the feeling of the energy," Elliot suggested.

I nodded and put all my focus on the stone circle. I took deep breaths and concentrated on feeling the heat from before warming me from the inside out. It didn't take long until I felt the heat inside, so I started imagining orange and yellow flames dancing around in the middle of the circle. I was concentrating so hard on keeping the energy hot and picturing what I wanted that my head started to ache. My chest burned intensely, and I felt that any moment I would burst into fire rather than the ground in front of me. I gasped and grabbed my head, losing focus on creating fire and tried to contain the pain instead.

"Serena? Are you ok?" Elliot asked concerned.

Without conscious thought, my mind reached out for water to quell the fire burning me inside but the access to both water and fire energy sent me into agony just as it did at the lake. It became hard to breathe as my chest constricted and my headache got worse. I doubled over and fell to the ground, thankfully not into the fire pit.

Elliot's voice sounded panicked, "Serena! What's happening?"

He knelt beside me and rested his hand on my back sending warmth and comfort through me, but it wasn't enough. I opened my mouth to scream but flames poured out. I quickly faced away from Elliot and sent the fire roaring toward the center of the stone circle. Eventually I quit breathing fire, but my body started to shake with tremors.

"Not quite what I was imagining," Elliot joked. At my drawn face his smile dropped. "We have to get you back to the nurse." Elliot stood up and reached down to pick me up.

Panda jumped in front of him and bleated. I was still doubled over but could see the struggle between Panda and Elliot. Avoiding his attempts to move her out of the way, Panda ducked under my chin and snuggled in underneath me.

Baa Panda bleated and nuzzled her lips against my cheek.

Suddenly the energies clicked inside and stabilized. Miraculously, I was holding both water and fire energy in my body and it was not tearing me apart anymore. I slowly straightened my body into a sitting position and breathed deeply, feeling the opposing forces shift and slide within. It was a weird feeling, but it also felt right.

Elliot's face looked ashen and his spiky hair was disheveled as if he ran his hand through it multiple times in stress. "Serena? Are you ok?"

I scrunched my eyebrows and titled my head, trying to figure out an accurate answer. The feeling inside me felt wiggly but stable. "I think I am ok now. I accessed the fire energy then the water and it felt like they were tearing each other apart inside my body."

Elliot nodded and sighed. "I was afraid of that. Fire and water are natural opposites. Having them both can't be good for you. Although, it looked like Panda helped calm you."

I looked to the baby goat nestled on my lap. If it really was Panda that helped stabilize me then having a familiar would have some benefits after all. Now, hopefully, I could practice freely without pain. I ran my hand down Panda's back letting the calm she brought wash over me from her presence. The energies inside finally disappeared leaving my body feeling normal.

"I think you should see the nurse," Elliot suggested. Before I could oppose the idea, he rushed out, "For me please. I want to make sure you are one hundred percent better."

I sighed. "Fine I will go." I ignored Elliot's offered hand, choosing to hold on to Panda instead. I wasn't ready to let go of her yet, too afraid the searing pain would return if I did. "I will see you tomorrow," I said softly to Elliot.

He gave me a small smile and waved but concern still shown in the tight lines around his smile and the small crease between his brows. I made a wide berth around Moto and made my way to the nurse's office, feeling embarrassed for the third time in front of Elliot.

The halls were quiet when I entered the school making the squeak of my shoes extra loud. It was nearly dinner time, so I wanted to hurry and get this examination over with. The door to the nurse's office was cracked open telling me she hadn't left yet. Laneli's whiny voice drifted out from the office, making me pause by the door. I really did not want to walk in while she was inside.

"I have been hearing rumors of something in the water," Laneli said.

I remembered hearing those same rumors, but why did Laneli care? Was she scared? The idea amused me. I imagined Laneli meditating near the lake as something rose from the water and grabbed her, pulling her into the lake with it. The horror and fear on her face would be priceless. I leaned forward to hear better.

"Alright, I guess we can check it out tomorrow. I will send someone to the lake and if there is something then they will take care of it. Just make sure you are nowhere around the lake at that time," the nurse replied in her ultra-chipper voice.

"Fine," Laneli responded.

I imagined an eye roll accompanied that one word. I heard heels clacking toward the door, so I scrambled back to the other side of the hall. When the door was yanked open, blue eyes full of attitude looked me up and down.

"Goat girl," Laneli commented, crossing her arms.

I think it was a greeting but couldn't be sure. She didn't ask about what I was doing in front of her mother's office or wait for me to give a response. Instead, she walked down the hall toward the doors leading to the quad. I let out a breath that I hadn't realized I was holding until then and gave Panda a little squeeze in relief.

"Now for a check-up," I told Panda as I walked into the nurse's office.

The nurse had her back to me, so I knocked on the door to announce my presence. She moved from side to side and nodded her head as if she was jamming to music. It didn't look like she heard me. Panda let out a loud cry, sounding just like a screaming baby, that caused the nurse to spin around with wide eyes, holding a hand to her chest. It wasn't the way I was intending to get her attention, but it worked all the same. She had earbuds in but quickly took them out and pressed pause on her phone.

"You scared me!" She took a deep breath and pasted on a bright smile to hide the startlement. "What can I do for you?"

Nurse Lydia wore her usual bright pink lipstick and heavy mascara. The blue eyes that peered at me reminded me of Laneli's, and I involuntarily shuddered.

"I sorta had an incident again, this time during training," I looked down at Panda embarrassed.

The nurse titled her head in confusion. "Incident? What do you-" Her eyes widened in realization. "Oh, I remember. You're the dual myth girl, right?"

Can't anyone in that family get my name correct? "Yup that's me. Can you see if I am ok?"

The nurse nodded and guided me to a nearby bed. I put Panda on the floor while the nurse put the ear tips of her stethoscope in her ears and put the other end against my chest to listen to my heart. After a moment she took her ear tips out and checked my pulse and temperature.

After I endured all her tests in silence, she finally told me my results, "You are fine, ducky!"

"That's it?" I didn't want her to suddenly realize something was wrong, so I jumped off the bed and walked to the door, gesturing for Panda to follow. I was glad that the examination was quick and successful. Now Elliot wouldn't have to worry. "Thank you, bye." This whole thing was a waste of time and my grumbling stomach told me too much time had passed since I put food in it.

"Hold on a second, dearie," the nurse called out.

Annoyance flared as I halted my progress to escape and turned slowly with a tight smile. "Yes?"

"Have you heard anything about a creature in the lake?" The nurse crossed her arms and studied me.

Did she know I overheard her conversation? I felt my palms start to sweat and my heart raced, making me want to run. "You mean like the loch ness monster?"

She let out a high-pitched laugh. "Don't be silly dear, the loch ness is in Scotland. I mean something else."

I bit my lip. I didn't know whether to comment on the fact that she practically admitted to the lock ness monster being real or just get the conversation over with quickly. Should I tell her what Marion told me about a naiad being in the water? My warning bells were going off. “No, I haven’t heard anything.”

“Ok, thank you anyway. Let me know if you hear anything.” She plastered on a bright smile.

I nodded and opened the office door, giving the nurse a small wave on my way out. Nurse Lydia waved back with her wide smile still in place. There was no way I would report anything to her unless it was about an injury or illness. I did not feel comfortable telling the mother of my enemy anything. I would rather go through Mr. Drakari.

I quickly sent Elliot a text saying I was cleared by the nurse. His reply of a smiling emoji was quick to appear. I took Panda to the cafeteria and grabbed some dinner then headed back to my dorm with a plate of chocolate cake in hand.

I opened the door to my room a crack and held the cake in front of me. “Peace offering?”

I waited until the plate left my hand before entering the room. Marion sat on her bed shoveling cake into her mouth and avoided my eyes.

“I’m sorry, Marion. I didn’t mean to yell at you.” I stuck my bottom lip out and raised my eyebrows until I was making what I hoped was good puppy dog eyes and a pleading expression. “Please forgive me.”

Marion set aside the plate and pounced at me, wrapping me in a tight hug. "Oh girl, there is nothing to forgive! I'm sure you had your reasons."

"Yeah, but my behavior was not acceptable." I hugged her back and took in a deep breath. "Let's go out on the lake tomorrow like you suggested."

I don't know where the idea came from, but it felt like the right thing to do. Marion was an excellent tutor and if she thought we should go out on the water then we should. I would have to pull up my big girl panties and get over my fear of water. Ha! As if my fear was going to go away that easily. However, I was sure if I had Panda and Marion there with me, I could deal with it and learn something useful.

Marion pulled back and looked at me with sympathy and forgiveness. "You don't have to do that."

I shook my head and held up a fist in determination. "No, let's do it."

Marion studied me, a slow smile spreading over her face. "Alright, tomorrow same time then. If you change your mind, don't be afraid to tell me."

I probably would change my mind, but I was going to do it no matter what.

Chapter 11

Attempted Myth-napping

"I'm going on a mission," Devon revealed at lunch the next day.

Marion squealed in excitement and shimmered into a clear form before becoming solid again. Her shout drew the attention of a few people at tables nearby.

Devon chuckled at his girlfriend's behavior and calmed Gus who started flapping at the sound. "Yeah, apparently there is a possible griffin blessed on the outskirts of the state, so Mr. Drakari is asking me to go." Devon beamed at us.

I was starting to realize that missions around here were the highest honor a student could receive. Plus, it was a way to get off campus for a while. I remembered my mission and how dangerous it could get.

"Be careful," I told Devon.

Devon smiled and waved my worry away. "Don't worry, I've been on missions before."

Devon was powerfully myth blessed and had a familiar to show for it, so it made sense that he had been called on before. Also, he had been at the school since thirteen so there had been four years that he could have gone on missions. I didn't know why I thought it was his first mission. I wondered if Marion had ever gone on one. She had been there the same amount of time as Devon but her lack of a familiar and over excitement whenever a mission was mentioned made me think she hadn't been.

"What's that I heard about a mission?" Harvey asked, setting his tray down next to mine and dropping his bag by his seat before sitting down.

Marion recapped the story excitedly, waving her hands and pointing to Devon multiple times. Harvey nodded as she spoke and took giant bites of his burger.

"Oh, right, I remember Laneli mentioning it and being upset that she was not invited on this one," Harvey commented with his mouth full.

I had forgotten about Harvey's task to follow Laneli around to make sure she was not misusing her powers. Last night's conversation between Laneli and her mother came to mind. Did Harvey hear it too, or was he off duty? I squinted my eyes at him trying to see if I could pick up the answer from his expression, but I was no mind reader.

Harvey gave me a hesitant smile. “Everything ok?”

I nodded my head and focused my attention back on my food. Staring at him wouldn’t do me any good. It would probably make him wish he made normal friends rather than weird staring ones. We spent the rest of lunch theorizing about how Devon’s mission would go until the bell rang, signaling the end of lunch.

“I will see you at our spot with a canoe,” Marion called out to me as she left, trailing after Devon.

I nodded to let her know I heard and tried to control the panic that caused my heart to race. I needed to go out on the lake to learn about my gifts and to control my fear. Before I could do that, I needed to get through gym. I headed to my next class looking for Elliot along the way.

Gym was tiring as usual but thankfully we did not do anymore battles using our myth blessed gifts. I was not ready to be barbequed again, or worse, barbecue someone else with fire breath. Elliot kept a careful eye on me throughout class, but I kept waving away his concern.

“I’m fine!” I told Elliot annoyed after the fifth time of him asking.

He held up his hands in surrender. “I’m sorry, I just don’t want to see you hurt.”

“Why?” I asked, my cheeks heating and heart racing at his confession.

His own cheeks reddened slightly, and he rubbed his arm. "Uh, you know, because I'm your tutor."

I felt my stomach drop in disappointment and my cheeks felt even hotter but this time in embarrassment. "Right, my tutor."

The coach blew his whistle calling an end to class. I turned quickly to hide my fallen expression and walked toward the lake calling over my shoulder, "See you later."

"Serena, wait-" Elliot called out to me, but I rushed away not letting him finish.

What was I thinking? For a second I thought Elliot was concerned because he was my friend or even liked me. I shook my head, feeling foolish. He had only known me for a couple weeks and had not hung out with me outside of tutoring or gym. I should have gotten the hint by now. I really needed to be on guard around him, especially since I kept embarrassing myself in his presence. I rounded the corner of the water wing and stopped when I saw the canoe by the lake. Seeing the canoe replaced all thoughts of Elliot with terror and dread.

I looked down at Panda who stared back with her adorable baby goat face. "Should we make a run for it?" I asked her half joking.

"Serena!" Marion called out, ruining my chance of a quick and unnoticed escape.

She wore her russet brown hair in pigtails with glitter to make her hair sparkly and sported a pair of shorts and a simple tank top. I looked down at my denim pants and white t-shirt, wondering if I should have gone back to my dorm to change into a more water appropriate attire first. Too late now.

Taking a deep breath and clenching my fists in an attempt at bravery I walked over to my friend and tutor, making sure Panda followed since I would need her to stabilize my energies. The canoe was larger up close. I inspected it for any holes and kicked it to make sure it would not fall apart.

"You ready?" Marion asked amused at my inspection.

My answer was in the form of tentatively getting in the boat and sitting on a bench in the middle, away from the edges as much as possible. Panda hopped in after me and took shelter underneath my bench. Marion pushed the canoe off the shore before getting in which rocked the boat. I gripped the edges of my seat trying to breathe and stay calm, though the rocking of the canoe terrified me. Marion sat across from me and grabbed a couple of oars, maneuvering us out to deeper water. When we were far enough from shore, she let the boat drift and put her hands in her lap. I stayed tensed and continued gripping my seat.

Noticing my discomfort, Marion gave me a hesitant smile. "Let's try to meditate first."

We both closed our eyes and opened our mind to the water, the sounds of birds, and the wind around us. It helped relax me to the point where I didn't need to grip the bench anymore, but I was still aware of the water surrounding us. When I felt at ease and in tune with the lake, as much as could be expected at least, I opened my eyes.

"Now what?" I asked, breaking the silence while I avoided looking at the rippling lake.

"Now we do what we have been trying to do for the past few days. Move the water." Marion gestured to the lake around us.

As a demonstration, Marion's body went translucent as she waved her hand over the lake. A small funnel of water rose up and circled around the boat before she moved it back to the lake and reformed her physical body.

I clucked my tongue at the display and went for sarcasm. "I don't know if I can make my body do that. That is more of a water sprite thing."

Marion rolled her eyes at me. "Just move the water."

I scooched over to the edge of the canoe slowly and peered over the side at the dark water. I saw my wide eyes and my wavy chestnut hair fanning my face in my reflection. Trying not to imagine how deep the water was or what could be swimming around underneath us, I faced Marion and took a deep breath.

"First I want you to try with only water energy," Marion advised.

I centered myself and opened the pathways to connect to the water energy, letting it flow through me. I made sure not to think about summoning heat or fire. I shuddered just thinking about what could happen if I were to spew fire at our boat.

When I felt as connected as I could be, I waved my hand at the water, imagining it rising like Marion made it do. I expected some cool water wave or funnel to swirl around now that I finally made it onto the lake, but nothing happened. I would have been happy with just a small disturbance in the water, but nope. I flapped my hand at the water, willing the water to move but it stayed calm underneath us.

I frowned and crossed my arms. "I guess I'm a dud." I moved back to the middle of the bench, thoughts of accidentally capsizing the boat driving a bit of fear back into my mind.

Marion held up a finger. "Hang on a moment. We still have to try blending the elements."

My heart raced at her suggestion. "What if I burn the boat? We will either burn, or sink, and who knows what is in this lake!" I rushed out, feeling a sense of panic overwhelm me.

Marion reached out and clasped my shoulders, making me look in her pale eyes. "One, I believe you will not do that. Two, we are both blessed by a water myth so we can probably breathe under water."

I narrowed my eyes. "Probably?"

Marion shrugged a shoulder. "I've heard about that being a thing but have never tested it."

I rolled my eyes and reached for Panda hiding under my seat. If I was going to attempt blending elements again, I would do it holding my stabilizing familiar. When Panda was settled in my lap I stared out at the lake and concentrated on blending fire and water energy. My chest began to ache, but the pain was manageable, and no headache appeared. Everything began to feel right inside as if I finally figured out all the secrets to my gifts. I even felt like I understood the myths that blessed me. I felt a force flow through me as I waved my hand at the lake and imagined forming a funnel of water. Marion and I held our breaths and waited to see the results.

A minute passed but no water moved.

"Well, that was underwhelming," I said disappointed, staring out at the lake in the last hope that water would rise at my command.

Marion let out a sigh. "I really thought that would work. I felt your connection to both elements, so I don't know why you are not able to control water."

I released my hold on the energies and put Panda back down on the floor of the boat. "Let's just head back to shore." After all my progress in blending energies and feeling connected, I had nothing to show for it.

"Hold on, we should try one more thing," Marion suggested.

I titled my head up to the sky and sighed. "We have tried everything."

"Well, maybe we should change what our outcome is."

I looked back at Marion who was smiling mischievously at me. "Uh oh, what are you thinking?"

Marion held out her hands, trying to calm me even though she hadn't told me what her plan was yet. "Now don't freak out."

"About what?" I asked hesitantly. I didn't like the tone she was using. She was obviously going to say something that made me in fact 'freak out.'

"I think we should try to test the theory about breathing under water. I will even join you." Marion bit her lip waiting for my reaction.

My jaw dropped at her suggestion. I looked over the edge of the boat at the dark, deep water and shook my head vehemently. "No, I'm good. I will stay here while you try it." I made a shooing motion with my hands, indicating for her to go ahead without me.

"C'mon Serena!" Marion pleaded, then she said in an authoritative tone, "I'm your tutor and I say we should try it together." She even put her hands on her hips and gave me a stern frown.

I shook my head and blinked slowly, amused at her show of authority but not at all moved by it. I crossed my arms in defiance and gave her a look that silently asked what she was going to do about it. Before Marion could try to convince me, a shriek sounded from the shore.

Our heads whipped to the side to look at what caused the sound. A struggle ensued on the lake shore between a girl and two beefy, thug looking men. I couldn't tell from that distance who they were, but I knew the girl was in trouble.

"Marion, we need to get to shore! Now!" I shouted, keeping my eyes on the struggle.

Marion grasped the oars and thrust the ends into the lake, pulling and pushing as fast as she could but it did not look like we would get there in time. One of the men pulled out a net and flung it over the girl while the other one used a rope to wrap around the net and secure it in place.

"C'mon, faster," I urged.

"Hey, I'm doing my best here," Marion shouted.

My eyes were riveted on the struggle and I leaned toward the shore as if it would help me get there faster. Why wasn't anyone helping her? Couldn't others hear her shrieks? I felt helpless.

Except we weren't helpless!

I conjured my fire and felt a rush of heat fill me. When it got too much to bear, I opened my mouth aiming for the attackers as flames poured out. It was the fastest conjuring of my gifts I had ever done. We were too far away for my fire to do any harm, but it got the men's attention. Unfortunately, the threat of fire made them go faster. One of them finished up with the rope and the other picked the girl up and threw her over his shoulder.

A stream of water flew by me and attacked the man carrying the girl in the net. I turned to Marion and saw her smile in triumph as she continued rowing. Two more streams of water flew by and attacked the two men. I knew Marion was trying to stop them from leaving and buy us some time to reach shore, but I could tell she was tiring.

"Let me row, and you continue the barrage." I waved my arm, telling her to move.

We quickly traded places and I put all my strength into rowing and getting us to shore as quickly as possible. Marion continued to throw water at them, her body shifting from physical to translucent and back. The men were now dragging the trapped girl since they couldn't pick her up in the onslaught of water.

"Serena, you are going to have to sing. We are close enough for them to hear you and I cannot keep this up for much longer." Her attacks began to slow, and the amount of water being thrown lessened, proving her point.

I growled at the situation. I hated the idea of taking someone's will but even I had to admit that it was necessary in that case. If we didn't stop them, then that girl would be long gone by the time we were able to run after them.

I kept rowing but I switched part of my focus to replacing the fire energy with water. The energy came readily. "Marion, cover your ears." I didn't wait to see if she followed my order. I opened my mouth and started singing.

My voice carried across the water, and I could only hope that no one else besides the kidnappers were in range. The melody was haunting as usual but held undertones of panic and anger. The men on shore abruptly halted and stood like statues awaiting orders. I rowed the rest of the way until our canoe bumped along the shore. Marion and I hopped out and surrounded the two men, blocking their route of escape although it didn't matter because they were in a trance. The girl in the net made a noise drawing our attention to her. We rushed over, quickly untied the rope and untangled the net from around her.

Are you ok?" I asked once the net was off and she was free.

The girl scrambled back and stared at us with wide, terrified eyes. I put my hands up to show her I meant no harm. Something odd struck me about her. A moment later I realized it was because she wasn't in a trance like the kidnappers.

As if reading my mind, Marion sucked in a surprised breath. "I knew it."

I didn't take my eyes off the scared girl in front of me, but I directed my question to Marion. "Knew what?"

Marion leaned over and whispered, "I think she is a naiad."

I looked over the girl trying to find how Marion knew. She wasn't affected by my singing. The girl was young and had long black hair with water lilies placed in it. Her clothes looked like simple coverings, not something I've seen anyone wear normally, and she was barefoot. Her eyes were blueish green that matched the color of the lake. However, my focus was drawn to her hands and ears. In between her pale fingers was webbing, most likely to help her swim better, and her ears were pointed. They were subtle differences but enough to make me believe Marion.

"Hello," I said to the naiad, "can you tell me what happened?"

The naiad looked between us then glanced at the enchanted abductors. She stood up and raced to the water without answering.

"Wait!" Marion and I called out.

The naiad stopped at the lake's edge. Glancing over her shoulder the naiad said in a soft voice, "Thank you," then dove into the lake, disappearing faster than I could track.

"Wow, that was amazing! I have never seen a real mythological being. Well, if you count your friend Tamara then I have but I mean out of normal society." Marion was jumping up and down in glee.

I chuckled at her enthusiasm and placed my hand on her shoulder to stop her bouncing. I shared her enthusiasm though. It was amazing to see the myth in the lake that people talked about. I turned my attention to the men who attempted to kidnap, or myth-nap, the naiad. How did they get on campus? How did they know about the naiad? Where were they taking her?

"We need to talk to Mr. Drakari," I told Marion.

She nodded in agreement but sucked in a breath. "What if he left for the mission already?" Marion asked.

I forgot that he and Devon were heading out today to find a griffin blessed kid. My eyes widened at the possibility. "We have to get a hold of him!"

"I'm going to go check the office. I will be back," Marion raced off toward the school leaving me by the lake with the two criminals.

I walked around them, trying to figure out their identities. Panda somehow knew that they had done something bad and headbutted one of the men's legs. I chuckled at my silly goat. The men were older, maybe in their late thirties or early forties. They didn't look like any teachers I had seen around. They were decked out in all black and had a backpack with them that I assumed used to hold the net and rope. I looked toward the quad, but no one appeared so I bent down and rifled through the backpack. Guilt surged through me since I was digging through someone else's property, but it was the only way that I could get a clue about their identities.

I found trail mix, binoculars, a recording device and a phone. I was about to pull out the phone and check the recent calls but a noise from the quad stopped me. I spotted Marion and Mr. Drakari walking my way urgently so I quickly zipped up the backpack and stood up. I was relieved to see that Drakari had not left on his trip yet.

"I heard you two fended off a kidnapping," Drakari said when he reached me. He looked over the two men who stood like statues and nodded approvingly at me.

"They captured a naiad in a net. I don't know who they are," I responded.

Drakari tapped his chin and circled the two men. "A naiad you say. Where is she now?"

"She jumped back into the lake," Marion responded.

"They have a bag with them. Maybe that will give you some clues." I pointed to the backpack next to my feet.

Drakari nodded and picked up the bag. "It already looks like the work of Hunters."

"Hunters?" I asked.

"Yes, a group of people that hunt mythological beings." Drakari looked unnerved. "Two of them on school property is unacceptable. I will have to call SMP right away."

"SMP?" I asked. I was starting to feel like a parrot.

"Society for Mythical Protection," Marion answered. "They help protect mythological beings and myth blessed."

Why was I the only one who didn't know these things? Ignorance was not fun.

"Thank you for what you did today girls. You helped save a mythological being and stopped two Hunters." Drakari gave us an approving nod and pulled out his phone.

Before he could dial, I asked, "What do Hunters do to myth beings?"

Drakari looked at me solemnly, "They kill them."

I frowned at his answer. "But-"

Drakari held up a finger, stopping me from making another comment, and spoke into the phone, "Hello, I need a team at the Colorado school immediately." He paused as the person on the other end spoke. "Mhm, two Hunters." He turned to look at the Hunters, "and bring a siren. Thank you." He hung up and turned to us.

"Sir, I don't think-" I tried again to tell him my thought, but he held up a hand stopping me.

"You two need to go now. I have this handled." Drakari gave us a look that left no room for negotiation.

I pursed my lips but did as he ordered. I looped my arm through Marion's arm and guided her back toward our dorm, making sure Panda followed.

"What were you trying to say?" Marion whispered to me.

I looked at her and frowned, my mind on the edge of something important. "It didn't look like the Hunters were here to kill the naiad. They looked like they were capturing her and trying to take her somewhere else."

Marion nodded slowly, remembering the struggle. "They did have nets and were dragging her away. I wonder why they were kidnapping her instead of killing."

Chapter 12

Fall Break Secrets

I never heard about what SMP did with the two Hunters and Drakari always sidestepped my questions about them. Eventually I stopped asking and continued my schooling with no further incidents. After two months, the lake event was the last thing I thought about. I was now able to create steam and warm myself with heat but still could not move water or fire despite practicing extra hard. It was disappointing. My tutors had tried to get me to touch fire or to breathe underwater but both ideas sent me into a fit of panic, so we never succeeded in attempting them. Thankfully, I wouldn't have to worry about training, my lack of skills, or school for one whole week due to fall break.

I sat in front of the school with my suitcase, watching countless parents drive by to pick up their kids while waiting for my own to arrive. A shadow fell over me making me look up at a tall spiky haired individual with a large Komodo dragon by his side.

"Mind if I sit here?" Elliot asked.

I waved my hand at the space next to me and moved Panda over to my other side. Elliot constantly told me Moto wouldn't eat Panda, but I didn't trust oversized lizards next to a baby mammal. We sat in comfortable silence for a while.

That awkward day at gym felt like ages ago and since then I had only ever held a professional relationship with him. My heart raced every time I saw him, but I had succeeded in hiding my feelings. Sitting this close to Elliot though, made all my silly feelings rush to the forefront. He smelled like a campfire and I loved the smell of campfires. He was also much more caring and sweeter when he was not faced against Laneli.

I curled my hands into fists, letting the nails dig into my skin and hoped it would help end the crush I had on my tutor.

"Excited for break?" Elliot asked unaware of my internal struggle.

I nodded my head. "You?"

Elliot shrugged and looked out over the cars flowing in from the gates. "It's just me and my mom, and she works a lot so break will be a bit boring."

"Do you have any siblings?" I imagined little Elliot's running around and thought his mom must have her hands full if that were the case.

“Nope. Well technically I have two half siblings, but they live in Michigan with my father, and I haven’t seen them in years.” Elliot’s face tightened and I couldn’t tell if it was in anger or sadness.

My heart broke for him. I couldn’t imagine being separated from my family for years. It would be nice to see him over break, so he was not so lonely, but he lived in northern Colorado and I lived in the opposite direction.

“Well, if you ever want to talk during vacation you know my number.” What was I doing? I should be avoiding him, not getting closer by offering to talk to him during break. Then again, there was nothing wrong with two friends talking.

Elliot nodded and gave me a genuine smile. My breath caught at how attractive his smile was and I found myself scooching closer to him. I was about to ask more about his life back home, but a honking car stopped me.

A gold van pulled up in front of us with my dad hanging out of the passenger side window. He held a camera and snapped pictures of everything in sight including students to my embarrassment. My mom got out of the van, which held up the entire line of cars behind her and walked over to me beaming.

“Oh honey! I finally get to see you after all this time! How is school and training. Ooo have you breathed any more fire or sung to a group of people?" My mother held out her hand to Elliot. "And who are you?"

My mother gave me a sly smile and waggled her eyebrows before giving Elliot her full attention. My cheeks burned, mostly because Elliot saw the look my mom made, too. My mother thought she was secretive with her insinuation, but it was as if she broadcasted her thoughts to everyone in the vicinity.

Elliot smiled politely but I could tell he was fighting a grin at my mother's behavior. "I'm Elliot."

"Are you chimera blessed too? I figured not a siren because those are always female, and you smell like a campfire so-" My mother was in one of those moods where she wanted to talk everyone's ear off.

"Mom!" I interrupted. Even though she was right about him smelling like a campfire, I didn't think pointing it out was polite.

Elliot looked amused by all of it. "I'm actually dragon blessed."

My mom's eyes widened, and she looked like she was about to faint. "Jared! This boy is dragon blessed!" My mom called over her shoulder to my dad.

My dad swiveled his camera over to us and took a picture of Elliot and me. I quickly stood up and walked over to the car with my suitcase and tugged the camera away from my dad. I was beyond embarrassed and the only sane thing to do was disappear.

"Mom, let's go," I said a bit forcefully.

I opened the side door and stuffed my suitcase in the van then urged Panda to hop in. That got my mom's attention and she hurried over to make sure my goat didn't eat her seats despite telling her over and over the past couple of months that Panda didn't go around eating everything in sight. I was sure my cheeks were still red when I turned back to Elliot who grinned in amusement. I waved goodbye and got in the van, quickly closing the door so he couldn't see me. My mom called out to Elliot as she got back into the driver's seat, wanting a last glimpse at the rare myth blessed. Elliot gave us all a wave, but his gaze seemed fixed on me despite the tinted windows.

Honking cars behind us finally got my mom to realize she was holding up the line. She gave one last wave to Elliot and drove away from the school. I hoped Elliot would forget all my parents' embarrassing actions so I wouldn't have to face his comments after break.

The car ride was an hour long and my mom and dad talked nonstop the entire way. Two familiar faces greeted me when we arrived, causing a deep sense of homesickness to flood my body. I threw open the car door and ran to them, tackling my two best friends with hugs.

"Oh, my goodness, it is so good to see you!" Rae squealed. It was nice to see her hair was just as orange and poofy as usual.

I glanced at Tam, silently asking if Rae knew about her identity but Tam shook her head. I would have to talk to her about telling Rae since keeping secrets from my best friend felt wrong. Panda trotted up to us and bleated, causing Rae and Tam to jump back at the sound. I laughed at them and knelt beside the goat. I had been on the receiving end of Panda's cries before and the eerie humanness of them startled me every time.

"Is this Panda?" Rae asked, leaning down to pet the black and white baby goat.

"Yup, my familiar." Even though my familiar ended up being a goat, I had grown fond of Panda. She was starting to get bigger, though, so I would have to find better accommodations soon.

"Tell me about everything," Rae said excitedly, and sat on the swinging bench on my porch.

Although I had kept in contact since I went to the Academy, Rae still wanted to know everything about my experiences there. Tam sat beside Rae on the bench swing waiting for me to recap the last two and a half months of school. I waited for my parents to go into the house before taking a seat on the porch floor next to Panda and telling them about everything.

I explained my first day including singing to save someone from drowning, and the different people I met. Tamara blushed when I mentioned Harvey's name which made me wonder if she secretly liked him. That would make Harvey happy. I told them about my classes, my first mission, meeting Panda, and learning about my dual myths.

"That story never gets old!" Rae exclaimed, referring to my incident at gym where I breathed fire on Elliot.

"So, what's up with you two. Anything you want to share?" I aimed the question at Tamara, hoping she would fess up to being a myth.

Tamara studied her purple nails, ignoring my pointed look. Rae looked between us both picking up on some unsaid message and grinned.

"Oh, I know what Tam is hiding, so you two don't need to be all secretive about it," Rae said mischievously.

Tam and I both froze. Did Rae figure out Tam was a djinn?

Rae smiled triumphantly. "C'mon girls. I know Tam has a secret boyfriend."

My eyes widened further, and a bubble of laughter threatened to escape. Rae assumed Tam had a boyfriend this whole time. I looked at Tam to share my amusement, but her face looked stricken. My smile widened at the realization that Rae was onto something.

"Where did you get that idea?" Tam asked incredulously.

Rae crossed her arms and gave Tam a knowing look. "I've seen you trying to hide your texts sometimes. Sneaking off to talk to someone or meeting up with someone when your parents think you are at my house."

"You do have a boyfriend, don't you?" This time I started laughing. "Who is it?"

Tam frowned and crossed her arms. "It's none of your business."

Her almost confession made Rae and I squeal in excitement. A smile broke out on Tam's face as she pushed away our hugs. "Can we go back to talking about Myth Blessed Academy and not my love life?"

I clicked my tongue, deciding to let the matter drop for now. "Fine, but I want to meet him before I leave."

Rae nodded, agreeing with me but Tam rolled her eyes. I couldn't tell if rolling her eyes was an agreement or a no-way gesture. Either way I would get her to reveal it one way or another. Poor Harvey though, this news might push him further into the shadows. He had been vying for her attention for almost three months now.

We talked all evening and Rae and Tam ended up staying the night. We also played with Panda and I showed them my trick with steam. Overall, it was a great first day of fall break, and something I sorely needed.

Throughout the week I hung out with my friends and had to spend time with my parents. Apparently, Rae had a weeklong plan of stuff to do until I had to go back including movie marathons, escapades through downtown and hitting all our normal hang out spots. I was fine with everything except for karaoke. I did not want a repeat of the last time. My parents kept inviting our neighbors over to see their myth blessed daughter which became awkward. I felt like a prize they had won that needed to be shown off to everyone.

The end of the week was near and I finally had a chance to relax. No running around town. No shaking hands and fake smiling. Just sitting and hanging out with my friends at the Tea House. The smell and taste of hot tea always soothed me and just entering the Tea House relaxed me. Rae and Tam were discussing, although I would say arguing, whether the original 1998 or the new 2018 Charmed show was better. My mind wasn't into the discussion, so I looked around our familiar hang out spot trying to take it all in before I had to leave. Not much changed except for the addition of a new barista and a new arcade game in the back.

I was staring at the arcade in the back and noticed a disturbance in the shadows. I peered closer, noticing a humanoid figure standing in the corner near one of the arcade games. The sight unnerved me, and I decided to check it out in case it was dangerous to the people in the Tea House.

"I will be right back," I told my friends.

They barely acknowledged my comment and continued arguing. I got up and creeped closer to the arcade area, glancing over my shoulder to make sure no one else was around.

When I saw the shadows shift again, it reminded me of someone. I whispered, “Harvey, is that you?”

I really hoped it was him otherwise I didn’t know what I was going to do. Then again, why would Harvey be there? The rumors of his stalking and creeping came to mind but I immediately discarded the idea. Harvey was a good person and I’ve known him long enough to know he wouldn’t do that.

I hope.

The shadow materialized into Harvey who wore his usual black clothing with dark hair hanging in front of half his face. He looked surprised to see me.

I gave a sigh of relief. “What are you doing here?” My relief turned to concern, and I gasped. “Did something happen to Marion? Elliot? Mr. Drakari?” I awaited his answer anxiously.

Harvey seemed hesitant and uncomfortable. He shifted and stuffed his hands in his pockets. “No, nothing is wrong with them-” He tilted his head at me and smirked. “Wait, Elliot? Since when do you-? Never mind, nothing is wrong.” He glanced over my shoulder and bit his lip. “I should go.”

I glanced over my shoulder to see what he was looking at but Tamara and Rae still discussing animatedly about Charmed were the only ones in sight. I looked back at him suspiciously. Maybe I didn’t know him as well as I thought I did.

“Are you stalking Tam?” I accused.

Harvey looked horrified and stuttered, "Wh-what? No, of course no- c'mon I wouldn't do that."

I stared at him a second longer, studying his face but found nothing concerning. I believed him but that still did not explain why he appeared and kept glancing at Tam. It was time Harvey was told about Tam's boyfriend so he would not keep pining after her. I opened my mouth to tell him and hopefully let him down easy, but his eyes widened, and he cursed. Harvey hunched his shoulders, trying to hide behind me. I shook my head, confused about his actions and turned to see what made him react that way.

Tamara stared at me with wide eyes and looked between me and Harvey, who was not doing such a good job at hiding. Tam whispered something to Rae then got up and rushed over to us.

"What are you doing?" Tam whisper-shouted at Harvey, sticking her finger out at him and ignoring me.

Harvey's stance relaxed and he gave Tam a flirty smile. "I wanted to see you. You weren't answering any of my messages."

My mouth gaped open and my eyes widened in realization. Harvey was Tam's secret boyfriend! How did that happen? When did that happen? I needed answers right now.

I smiled like an idiot, trying to control my laughter in case it drew unnecessary attention. "You," I pointed to Tam, "and you?" I pointed to Harvey and clapped my hands quietly in excitement. This was the cutest and most amazing thing I had heard since finding out our local ice cream shop had huckleberry flavor.

Tam grabbed my hands to stop me from clapping. "Shh, you weren't supposed to find out like this."

"I told you we shouldn't keep it secret from her." Harvey smirked at the situation and crossed his arms, obviously not agreeing to Tam's desire to keep their relationship secret.

Tam glared at me and Harvey then threw her hands up in the air. "You two are too much."

"Who are you two talking to?" A voice asked from behind us.

Tam froze and closed her eyes, probably wishing she could disappear. I turned and grinned at Rae.

"This is Tam's boyfriend, Harvey," I introduced, finding so much amusement in the situation. "He is from Myth Blessed Academy."

Rae's eyes lit up and she did the same quiet clapping that I did before.

Harvey held out a hand in greeting. "You must be Rae. I've heard a lot about you."

"You better have," Rae joked and clasped his hand in greeting.

Harvey raised her hand to his lips, placing a soft kiss on her knuckles like he did to Tam and me when he first met us.

Rae looked like she was going to swoon, but her excitement soon morphed into curiosity. “How did you two meet?”

I sucked in a breath. Oh no, I may have messed up. Tam couldn’t tell Rae that she met him when she went to see me the first week of school. Rae would either question how Tam got there or why she wasn’t brought along. Either one could reveal that Tam was a djinn. I glanced guiltily at Tam who pursed her lips and gave me a small frown.

“Well-” Harvey started but drifted off not knowing what to say.

I titled my head at him but looked at Tam questioningly, wondering if Harvey knew about her being a djinn. She gave me a small nod. My eyes widened at the news. Why did she tell Harvey but not Rae?

Tam closed her eyes and pinched the bridge of her nose, letting out a deep sigh. Tam looked up at Rae sadly. “There is something I need to tell you.”

Harvey and I reached out a hand to Tam. “You don’t need to do this,” we told her simultaneously.

Tam looked at all three of us with a small smile and straightened her shoulders. “Yeah I do. She is my best friend and I have kept it hidden for too long. I trust you guys.”

“Ok, what is going on?” Rae demanded, putting her hands on her hips.

Instead of saying anything, Tamara held out her hands and purple smoke drifted around them. The smoke disappeared and in its place was a cup of tea. Rae stepped back in astonishment.

"What-" Rae started but was too shocked to say more.

Tam moved her hands and dropped the cup of tea. Rae and I reached out for it to stop it from breaking, but the cup was engulfed in purple smoke again and returned to Tam's hands. Harvey became shrouded in purple smoke and when it disappeared, he was in bright yellow pants and an orange T-shirt. I clapped my hand over my mouth to stop from bursting out in laughter. Harvey looked down at his clothes and groaned.

"How many times have I told you to stop doing that?" Harvey scolded Tam and stared disgustedly at the colorful garments he wore.

Tam chuckled and returned him to his dark, goth look. Rae stared at us like we had jumped off the deep end.

"So…I'm a djinn," Tam revealed as if her displays weren't enough.

Rae continued to stare at her with a slack jaw and wide unbelieving eyes. I poked her to make sure she wasn't accidentally frozen, and her head spun to stare at me.

"And you have known about this for how long?" Rae asked, sounding hurt.

I hunched my shoulders guiltily. “About three months.”

Rae shook her head and laughed in disbelief and annoyance. “The best secret ever and you guys kept it from me?”

“Rae…” Tam started but didn’t finish.

It must have been hard to keep that kind of secret from her friends, but it was a life or death situation. If that secret fell into the wrong hands, then Tamara could be enslaved forever. Thinking about it more, I was surprised she revealed it to me and my roommate.

Rae waved her hands at us and grinned. “It’s ok, I figure you have your reasons.”

Tam and I blinked at her in surprise. We had expected more anger or disappointment or… something. Then again, this was Rae we were talking to. Rae of sunshine her family and friends called her because of her constant positivity.

“This is so cool! My best friend is a djinn and my other best friend is myth blessed!” Rae clapped excitedly. “So, tell me how you two met.” Rae pointed between Harvey and Tam.

Tam beamed, now that she knew her friend wasn’t upset with her. Tam explained how she visited me my first week and went to dinner with me and my friends. I knew everything up to the point when Harvey and Tam started hanging out. “One time I popped into Drakari’s office djinn style, but Harvey was there and saw the whole thing. I didn't sense him because of his shadow gift."

"We started talking and hanging out, then one day we decided to date," Harvey finished, looking fondly at Tamara.

"Awww," Rae and I exclaimed.

"Well, since you're here, I guess you can stick around," Tamara told Harvey nonchalantly.

I wasn't fooled. I could tell she was excited he was there.

The four of us walked away from our shadowy corner and out of the Tea House. We decided to go back to Tamara's house, so we piled into Rae's car and headed that way.

"You guys cannot tell anyone about my djinn identity or my relationship with Harvey," Tam ordered from the back seat. "My family and I could be in danger if anyone knew we were djinns and I would be in danger from my parents if they knew I was dating a myth blessed guy."

The idea of her parents finding out about her boyfriend was amusing but the thought of anyone discovering that she was a djinn worried me. My mind immediately went to Hunters and I shivered. Knowing how much Rae, Harvey, and I cared for her though,
I knew Tam's secret was safe.

Chapter 13

So Many Questions

Fall break ended too soon although hanging with my friends made it all worth it. I tapped my pencil against my book in my last class before lunch, thinking about the night I found out about Harvey and Tam. We had gone back to Tamara's house and played around with our powers until we were wiped out from all the energy spent. Rae was a good sport about everything and didn't feel bad for herself at all since finding out all her friends were either a myth or myth blessed. She had more spirit and happiness than anyone I had ever met.

Thankfully class ended without me getting in trouble for spacing out through most of it and I was free to go to lunch. Harvey met up with me outside of class and we walked together to the cafeteria. Marion and Devon were already at our usual table and Panda ran ahead to greet Gus. Looking at the familiars made me think about their purpose. Devon, Elliot and I had one because apparently, we were powerful. However, I had seen Harvey's powers at work and there was nothing like it, so why did he not have a familiar? I brought up the question to Harvey when we sat down, and Marion and Devon gave him curious stares, wondering the same thing.

"Well, Mr. Drakari once explained to me that pure spirit myths are not tied to animals since they are mainly incorporeal." Harvey smiled as a thought came to him. "I like to think of the shadows as my familiar."

"What about werewolf and vampire blessed?" Marion asked. "They are known to have familiars if they are powerful enough."

Harvey nodded, "Yes, but vampires and werewolves are not pure spirits. They have a physical body that has been changed so they often double dip into another element."

We nodded and ate our food, processing the information. I wondered how a person became powerfully blessed. Did it depend on when they were blessed or where they were when it happened? I would have to ask my Myth History professor sometime. My mind drifted to when I was blessed. I had never seen a chimera, but I was ninety percent sure I saw a siren at the time of my blessing.

"Have you ever seen a…" I struggled to pronounce the name of the myth he once told me, "Nalusa Chito or other mythological beings?" I asked Harvey.

Obviously, he shouldn't admit to Tam being a djinn, but I wondered if he ever saw anything else. Harvey looked calm and didn't even flinch at my question.

"Yeah, I saw a Nalusa Chito when I was six. My family lived in Oklahoma at the time. I am pretty sure it blessed me then, but I didn't come into my powers until I was thirteen." Harvey shuddered at the memory. "Those things are terrifying."

"What about you guys? Have you ever seen a myth?" I asked, bringing Marion and Devon into the conversation.

"Other than that naiad and your- well just the naiad, I haven't seen anything," Marion said.

She almost slipped up about Tamara. I would have to keep a close eye on my roommate. I didn't believe she would purposely tell people about Tam but maybe one of these days she may get over excited and slip up.

Devon tapped his chin as he thought about the question then shrugged. "I am pretty sure my next-door neighbor in Buena Vista was a troll, but there is no way to be sure."

We laughed at his comment and started joking about what type of being our peers and teachers would be if they were myths. A shy looking ten-year-old approached the table and held out a note to me. As soon as I took it, he ran off, probably terrified to be talking to seniors. Harvey peered over my shoulder to read it with me while Marion tried to read it upside down from the other side of the table.

Your presence is required in the nurse's office

I stared at the note curiously as I stood up then checked my watch. Lunch was about to be over so at least this would let me miss gym. "I wonder what this is about. I hope she didn't find something wrong with my latest results, like some late occurring illness or something."

Marion shrugged. "I don't know but make sure to tell me what happens."

I left the three of them at the lunch table and walked to the nurse's office with Panda. The door was open when I arrived, but I knocked anyway to announce my presence.

"Come in dearie and take a seat," The nurse called from within the office.

I slowly made my way in, noticing that the office was empty except for the two of us. Nurse Lydia was sitting at a desk near the door, so I took a seat opposite from her and made sure Panda laid by my side. The nurse stared at me as if waiting for me to say something, but I didn't know why I was there, so I stayed quiet.

"I wanted to ask you some questions," Nurse Lydia finally said. "It's routine after any break from the Academy."

No one mentioned having to answer questions after break. Maybe Marion and the others were so used to doing it they forgot that it wasn't normal for me.

"Ok, what did you want to ask me?" I nodded my head to let her know she could go ahead and ask.

Nurse Lydia studied a clipboard in front of her, then brought her gaze back to me. "Did you witness anything strange in your town?"

I tilted my head in confusion. "Strange?"

"Did you see anything that might indicate another myth blessed or even a mythological being in your town?" The nurse rephrased.

My mind immediately went to Tamara and her family but there was no way I was going to tell the nurse about them. "No," I lied.

The nurse studied me a moment, comparing my words to my actions. I must have succeeded at controlling my expression and movements because the nurse wrote something down on her clipboard and moved on.

"Have you ever seen a mythological being before, and if so, how many?" Nurse Lydia had a calm expression but the way she tapped her pen on the clipboard seemed to show impatience.

I had to think about this carefully. In reality, I had seen a siren, a djinn, and a naiad. Mr. Drakari knew about all three, but I didn't know if he told the nurse about them. If I answered differently than what she expected, then she would know I was hiding something. Safe bet would be that she knew about the siren and naiad, especially the naiad since it was on campus.

"Two, a siren and naiad," I answered.

Nurse Lydia marked the paper in front of her. "When did you see them and where?"

Drakari already knew everything, so why did I have to go through that line of questioning? Best thing to do would be to answer short and quick so I could hurry and leave. "The siren was in July in Hawaii, and the Naiad in August at the lake on campus."

The nurse looked surprised. "You saw the naiad here?"

I nodded and checked my panda watch. My tutoring session with Marion was soon. I did not want to miss it. I fidgeted in my chair hoping she would hurry and finish her questioning. Why was the nurse the one doing this anyway? A counselor or the principal would probably be more appropriate.

"I am going to need to take some blood and test it for any traces of magic," The nurse said calmly and stood to grab her equipment.

I frowned at her back. "Traces of magic, what do you mean?"

She returned with a needle and an alcohol wipe and started cleaning an area on my arm. "Whenever a mythological being is near they leave a trace of magic in a human's system, so I am going to check your blood."

At my concerned and wary look, the nurse chuckled. "Don't worry dear, it is for demographics and a census on magical beings."

I nodded slowly but the whole thing sounded odd. Then again, what did I know? I was new to all this myth stuff. I stayed still until she got the blood, she needed then quickly stood up so she couldn't take anymore. I wasn't exactly afraid of needles, I just didn't like the sensation of being pricked by one.

"So, how are your powers coming along?" The nurse asked sweetly as she put away the vial of blood and sat back at her desk.

Her change of subject surprised me. "Uh, good I guess."

"A dual myth blessed like you has never been heard of. What can you do?" The nurse looked nonchalant but her keen interest in my abilities was slightly disconcerting.

"Um, not much. I can create steam and heat. That's about it. Well other than singing and breathing fire." I checked my watch again, this time trying to signal the nurse that I needed to go.

She ignored my hint and asked another question. "Do you know how or why you were blessed by two myths?"

"I have no idea." That question had been something I had been pondering ever since I found out I was chimera and siren blessed. I shouldered my bag, signaling to her more obviously that I had to go.

Nurse Lydia stood up with me. “Thank you for answering the questions. I will send the report over to Mr. Drakari soon.” She walked me to the door and waved, smiling wide as usual.

I walked down the hall to the exit door quickly, wanting to escape before she asked any more questions. I would have to ask Marion and Elliot when they were due to be questioned and if meetings like that were always weird.

I made my way over to the lake, wanting to have enough time to talk to Marion and work on my nonexistent water affinity. Panda trotted by my side and danced around a few times on the quad as we walked. Marion was meditating and waiting in our usual spot, and Panda ran up to her vying for attention. I chuckled at the cute little goat and sat down in front of my tutor, crossing my legs and breathing in the lake.

“How did it go?” Marion asked, her eyes still closed.

I frowned at the topic. “The nurse wanted to ask me some questions then drew some blood to test. When is your appointment?”

Marion cracked her eyes open and peered at me. “She drew your blood? Why?”

Chills ran down my arms at Marion’s question. If it was not a normal thing to do after breaks, then why did she single me out? I thought of Tamara and our magic usage over fall break. Maybe the nurse thought I was showing outsiders secrets of the Academy. I would have to be more cautious out in the open, especially since my friend was a djinn.

I shook my head and shrugged. She let the topic go for the time being. We continued our training of trying to manipulate the water but the nurse's questions and the spot where she drew blood were still on my mind.

After practice, I focused on the ground as I walked to the campfire area where Elliot would be waiting, wanting to avoid tripping over rocks or Panda. My mind was also stuck on replay of the events over fall break. I finally found out why Harvey was so feared at school. For one, he could appear and disappear at will. However, the main reason was because a year ago, Harvey materialized through the shadow of a large boy scaring the boy so bad that he tripped and fell down an embankment which broke most of his bones. Most of the "witnesses" said that Harvey reached into the boy's shadow and crushed his bones. Harvey never corrected them. Rae had gotten a kick out of that story. I couldn't help but snort out a laugh at the image of Harvey purposely hurting someone through their shadow. I know that sounds bad, but it would take a lot to get Harvey upset and the idea that he would do that to someone for fun was ridiculous.

A nudge on my cheek frightened me and, thinking it was a cobweb, I swatted at it to make it go away. A flame rather than a cobweb floated away from me. The flame was strange, not just because it was floating but it also looked like a rose. I took a step closer to it and brought my hand up to cup the fire rose. I let out a quiet snort of disbelief when it fit perfectly into my hand without burning me.

Dancing lights in my peripheral made me look away from the fire in my hand to find the source. More floating fire roses dotted the air, making a path toward the side of the campus. I figured the fire roses wouldn't hurt me and I was curious about what was at the end of the path, so I followed the roses. The sight at the end of the line took my breath away. Floating roses made of fire dotted the air everywhere I looked and standing in the center was Elliot, smiling shyly at me.

"Did you do this?" I asked Elliot amazed.

"Do you like it?" He answered.

I spun around taking in all the beautiful lights. "I love it."

A rose drifted down to float between our chests. It was reflected in Elliot's copper eyes, making them glow.

Elliot took my hands and cupped them under the rose. "Try to touch it."

I already knew it wouldn't burn me, so I did as he told without an ounce of fear. The rose felt hot and feathery, tickling my hands as it burned in my palms, but I did not ever feel like it would hurt me. It was a nice change to the terror I usually felt toward touching fire.

"I guess you are immune to fire then," Elliot said softly, still holding my hands.

I lifted the rose above our heads, making it float above us. My cheeks hurt with how much I smiled. I had never seen such a beautiful sight and for once, I wasn't scared around the fire.

Elliot cleared his throat, drawing my attention to him. "I have to admit that I had a motive for making these roses other than testing your fire immunity." His cheeks reddened slightly, and he glanced away.

I had never seen Elliot look embarrassed before, but it was cute. "Then why did you make them?" I teased.

Elliot shifted his feet and stuck his hands in his pockets. "It is after fall break now. That means the Academy will be preparing for the Halloween dance."

My heart started racing. The fire roses were super romantic and now the mention of a dance. Was Elliot about to…

"I was wondering if you'd like to go with me," Elliot asked.

"To the dance?" I asked stupidly. I mentally shook my head. Of course, he meant to the dance. My heart fluttered and my cheeks heated but I chalked that up to the fire being so close to my body rather than the gorgeous dragon blessed asking me to a dance.

Elliot chuckled and nodded, tucking a strand of hair behind my ear, just like in a cliché romantic movie. I nodded my head in answer and jumped up and down excitedly. At his amused grin, I settled down and fidgeted with the strap of my watch.

“Why me?” I asked, feeling self-conscious. I never knew Elliot felt that way about me and it made me wonder why he would choose a siren blessed for his date to the dance.

Elliot titled his head and frowned. “Why not you?” When I didn’t respond, he stepped closer and rested his hands on my arms. “From the first moment I met you I knew you would be interesting. You are completely different than the other siren blessed. You care and you fight for what is right. I’ve gotten to be near you, to know you, in the last couple of months and have enjoyed every moment of it. I would like to spend more time with you if that is ok.”

My heart flip flopped at his confession and I had to look away before he saw how his words affected me. I knew he would be interesting when I first met him at the Karaoke place, and I had grown closer to him the longer we spent time together too, but I had always thought it was one sided.

I nodded enthusiastically. “I would like that.”

We spent the rest of our tutoring session playing with the fire roses and planning our date.

I think it was a date.

I didn’t realize how wide I was smiling or how goofy I probably looked until Marion mentioned it in our dorm room.

“You look like you just got hit with Cupid’s arrow,” Marion laughed. She was sitting at her desk with a journal and a math book in front of her.

I grew serious at her comment. “Is Cupid real?” Mythological beings were real so I shouldn’t be surprised if angels, demons, and gods were real too.

“No evidence of a real Cupid but we have seen too much to discount the possibility,” Marion said waving her pen in the air before bringing it back down to the page in front of her.

“So, what has you smiling like that?” Marion asked but stayed focused on writing notes in her journal.

“Elliot asked me to the dance,” I said with barely contained glee.

I never thought I would be one of those typical girls who got all giggly and ridiculous about being asked to a dance, but here I was doing exactly that. Marion jumped from her desk chair at my news and tackled me in a hug, her body going translucent in her excitement.

“Yay, Elliot finally asked you!” She squeezed tighter before finally letting me go.

I laughed at her enthusiasm. “Why do you say finally?”

Marion’s body became watery and see through again and she waved away my question. “Girl, please. I know you two have been crushing on each other for a while now.”

That was news to me. I thought Elliot saw me only as an acquaintance, a friend at most. I know he said his feud was with Laneli and the other sirens, but I always felt he held me at a distance because of my siren side. Especially when he found out my gifts worked on him despite his immunity.

"We should go shopping." Marion grabbed her purse and sprayed glitter into her pigtails. Once she was ready, she started dragging me to the door.

I pulled my arm back, halting her progress. "You want to go now?"

It was a school night and we had two weeks until the dance. I didn't understand the rush. Marion seemed offended that I would ask such a question and went to grab my arm again.

"Of course, now. I am so excited, and we need to get something before all the good dresses are gone." Marion started dragging me to the door, but I pulled back again.

"Fine but let me make a call first." I pulled out my phone and dialed.

Marion gave me a curious frown with her hands on her hips but smiled when she heard the voice.

"Hey girl! What's up?" Tamara asked from the other end.

I explained to her what Marion was making me do and why but before I could finish, purple smoke filled our room. When the smoke dissipated, Tamara was standing there in a ta-da pose. I stared at her then my phone which was still connected to her line. Finally, I ended the call and held out my hands upright wanting an explanation.

Understanding my silent question, she walked over to Marion and faced me. “I’m here to go shopping with you. Harvey and I are going to the dance, so I need a dress too.”

“Can’t you just,” I waved my hand in the air, “poof one into existence?”

“What’s the fun in that?” Tamara laughed. “So, who’s car are we taking?”

I guess I was going to town then. I looked over to my familiar who had already found a spot on my bed to sleep. There was no point in waking her to bring along.

“We don’t have a car. We were just going to walk,” I said, resigned to our adventure.

Tam frowned and pulled us in. “Hang on!”

Purple smoke surrounded us until I couldn’t see anything. I expected it to fill my mouth and nose with a pungent odor, but it was unscented, and I could still breathe easily. My stomach suddenly dropped like it did on a roller coaster then my feet thudded against something hard. The world spun around me and I stumbled, trying to get my bearings. The fading smoke slowly revealed a well-lit but dank alley.

I just teleported! It must be awesome to be a djinn.

Marion breathed heavily and braced herself against an alley wall. She looked at me with a wide smile and bright eyes. I knew that look. I had the same look on my face. It was a look that said we would do that again in a heartbeat despite being disoriented upon landing. Tamara waited with hands on her hips, giving us a second to recover. Once we had our balance back and our breathing back to normal Tam led the way to the mouth of the alley but hesitated not knowing where to go next. Marion picked up on her hesitation and shouldered her way to the front. She led us down a street to our first store which happened to be a Tibetan clothing shop.

Marion was an excellent guide, telling us stories about students in town or the history of the shops we passed. I loved the fact that local businesses made up most of the small town. A steam train passed through multiple times blowing its whistle loud for all to hear. Residents in Jeeps that were caked in mud drove by making me wish I was four wheeling rather than shopping.

By the time we reached the end of the street, Marion already had three bags and Tam had two small bags, but I hadn't found anything that I wanted to buy other than huckleberry ice cream.

"Maybe we should head back and try another day," I suggested hopefully. Don't get me wrong. I loved shopping but only in antique shops or odd stores. I was very picky when it came to clothes.

Tam hugged my arm. "No, you can't give up yet. We still have a few stores to check out." She stared at me with hazel-gray puppy dog eyes.

"One more," Marion pleaded.

I looked between them and sighed. "Fine. One more."

Marion and Tamara pumped their fists in happiness and raced off to the next store. I went to follow them but a brownish-red blur near an alley across the street caught my attention. My friends had already gone inside leaving me alone on the street, so I had no one to ask about what I saw. I assumed it was an animal. I didn't see any more movement from the alley, so I opened the door to the shop that Marion and Tam were browsing, ready to get on with the shopping. A small animal cry made me turn back to the alley. I would never forgive myself if I didn't help an injured animal. I released the door, letting it close on its own, and crossed the street.

I usually made it a habit to not enter creepy alleys after years of reading about them in books, but it looked like I was going to have to do it for the second time in a day.

I pressed my body up against the wall near the entrance to the alley and poked my head around to peer in. I figured it would be better to assess the situation first before blindly rushing in. Wild animals didn't take kindly to strangers in my experience. Memories of being forced into a room with various wild animals by my parents to test me for myth blessings threatened to overwhelm me. I shuddered at the memories and shoved them to the back of my mind, instead focusing on the here and now.

I forgot all about hiding and assessing the situation when I saw who was in the alley. Laneli stood with her knees bent and feet apart with her arms spread out as if blocking something from getting passed her. I stepped away from the wall and approached her from behind. When I tapped her on her back, Laneli screeched and jumped away. She must have been so focused on what was in front of her that she didn't hear me approach her. She scowled at me and crossed her arms, her blonde hair falling into her face and sweat dotted her brow.

My eyes widened at the creature Laneli was cornering. It was a brown and red fox, but the swish of its tail told me I was not looking at any ordinary fox. The small creature had two tails and looked between us with intelligence beyond any normal animal. During one of the times I had talked to him over the last couple of months, Ian once mentioned that kitsunes were Japanese spirit and fire myths that had multiple tails. The most powerful kitsunes had nine tails so I knew I was looking at a lower level one.

The kitsune made a run for it but Laneli was not as distracted as she seemed. She whipped out a net that landed over the kitsune, and it let out a cry. It was the same cry I heard before. The one that drew me over to the alley but now it was much louder and more frightened.

I rushed over to the kitsune. “What are you doing?” I shouted at Laneli, trying to tug the net away.

I was suddenly shoved from the side and fell back on the asphalt. My hands stung from skinning them, but I was too focused on freeing the myth to care. I stood up and knocked Laneli away from the net. She had been trying to lift the animal in it and carry it away but stumbled back when I shoved her.

“I am trying to take it to a secure location,” Laneli explained annoyed. Her blue eyes held determination and something else that made her look crazy.

Her words were innocent enough but that something else in her expression made me block her from the animal. I didn’t know what Laneli really wanted it for but there was no good reason she needed to take it away from its natural habitat. A silver glint alerted me of danger before Laneli charged at me. I dodged the attack, stunned that she would try to stab me. She used the same dagger I had seen her with the first time we met.

On instinct I opened my mouth and called out for Tam. I had no idea why I thought she could hear me, but it was worth a try. Tam was a powerful djinn after all. Purple smoke filled the alleyway and I took the opportunity to jump forward and release the kitsune while Laneli was distracted.

“You know you could have just called me on a phone like a normal person!” The voice spoke from the smoke. When it cleared, Tam stood there with Marion.

Laneli stared at us with an open mouth, glancing between the kitsune and the newcomers. Deciding she was outnumbered, Laneli darted to the end of the alley, escaping us before we could catch her.

Crap. I might have made a huge mistake.

Chapter 14

She Be Crazy

"What is going on here?" Marion asked, still holding on to Tamara.

Tamara hadn't moved since she discovered Laneli and I in the alley. She continued to stare at the spot Laneli used to be with unblinking eyes. I didn't blame her. I had just revealed her secret to an outsider and one who loved to abuse power.

"Laneli had a two tailed kitsune cornered and then tried to attack me with a dagger," I explained softly.

I stood a few feet from them with the net dangling from my fingers. The kitsune was long gone so the only thing I had to prove my story was the net and the fact that they had seen Laneli a few moments ago flee the scene. My head spun with questions about Laneli's motives and worry over Tam's predicament. Maybe If I sang to Laneli and forced her to forget, then Tam's secret would be safe. I mentally shook my head at the thought. I didn't want to take away people's free will, even if it was Laneli's will that I would be taking. However, I did have fire breath. I mentally smacked myself for not thinking of that sooner. Mr. Drakari would know what to do.

"I think we should go back to the school," I suggested, aiming the words at Tam.

A small frown was the only indication she heard me. I dropped the net and walked over to her slowly. Marion stood to the side watching our interaction with wide eyes. I placed my hands on Tam's shoulders and made her look at me. I could see hurt and anger in her hazel-gray depths causing my stomach to squeeze in guilt. I expected her to disappear and leave me alone to find my own way back to the school but what she did next surprised me.

Tamara wrapped me in a hug and whispered, "I'm glad you're ok." Then she grabbed Marion's hand, keeping one arm wrapped around my shoulders, and transported us away from the alley in a cloud of purple smoke.

I wasn't surprised to see that Dominic Drakari's office was where we appeared. Thankfully we didn't interrupt any meetings and Drakari was alone, writing in a journal at his desk. He glanced up at the three of us and put his pen down, studying us with a calm unsurprised expression.

The three of us started talking at once trying to get in our parts of the story but Drakari held up a hand, instantly silencing us. He was used to drama at the school and didn't react at our behavior.

"One person," he said, holding up a finger.

Marion and Tamara looked at me. It made sense that I should tell him since I saw more than they had. I stepped forward and rested my hands on his desk then immediately stood straight again when the scrape on my hands stung from falling against the ground. "Laneli attacked me with a knife."

Finally, Drakari's calm exterior cracked and he leaned forward with a deep, concerned frown. He pierced my gaze with his green eyes and for the first time I could see the werewolf blessing in them. "Tell me exactly what happened."

I explained everything to him from the moment we left the dorms, though he seemed uninterested in our shopping adventures, all the way to the moment we arrived in his office. His brows drew upward as I retold Laneli's actions and Tamara's revealed secret. Once I finished speaking, I collapsed in the high back chair across from his desk and waited for his response.

He glanced over the chair at Marion and Tamara before settling on me again. "This is truly alarming."

"Ya think?" I asked sarcastically.

Drakari ignored me and reached for the phone. He held it to his ear after dialing and we waited patiently, except for me who waited with a tapping foot, for Drakari to say something. “Come to my office.” He hung up the phone and regarded us. “Ms. Michaels will of course be expelled but the first order of business is getting your secret cleared up.”

A moment later, a guy dressed in all black stepped from the shadows in the corner of the office. “You rang?” Harvey asked. He took in all our serious expressions, his eyes landing on Tamara last. As soon as he saw the look of fear and anger on her face, he turned to Drakari with even darker, stormy eyes and clenched fists. “What’s wrong?”

Drakari didn’t react. I was starting to think Drakari had a special poker face for all the students at the Academy. “Where is Laneli?”

Harvey blinked, the fury leaving him instantly. He looked from Drakari to Tam and back. “She should be in her room.” Harvey seemed unsure now that we were staring at him with varying degrees of anger and concern.

Drakari leaned back in his chair. “Bring her here,” he ordered.

Harvey gave a fond look to Tamara before stepping into the shadows and disappearing. Once he was gone, Drakari spoke to Tam with a stern tone. “Go home and I will deal with this.” She was about to argue but Drakari’s words stopped her. “We can’t let Ms. Michaels see you when she arrives.”

Tamara frowned but acquiesced. I stood up wanting to say goodbye to my friend and apologize before she left but I came face to face with only smoke. I would call her later to talk. Hopefully she could forgive me for revealing her secret. A moment later, Harvey arrived with a wriggling, blonde she-monster in his grip. When she saw us all staring at her, she composed herself and strode over to the high back chair I was sitting in and stood by the arm. She glared at me before resting her gaze innocently on the principal.

"How can I help you?" She asked Drakari sweetly. Her tone made me want to punch her and pick up what we started in the alley.

"I have heard some very concerning things about the behavior you exhibited earlier today," Drakari stated, giving her a chance to confess.

Laneli's face hardened and a scowl replaced her sweet smile. It was like seeing an angel turn into a demon. "She was interfering in matters that don't concern her."

Drakari frowned at Laneli, the first emotion he expressed since I told him the story. "Tell me exactly what happened."

"I was trying to help a wounded animal-" she started.

I snorted, interrupting her explanation. There was no way trapping a mythological being with a net and terrifying it was helping.

Laneli glared at me before morphing her face into one of innocence. "I was just about to grab the animal to help it when Serena ran over howling and pushed me. I pushed her back then had to defend myself with a knife when she attacked me again. I barely got away when a strange smoke filled the area." Laneli's voice cracked in the end and she tilted her head down as if she was going to cry.

What kind of garbage was she spouting? That was not how everything went down at all! I never attacked her first, and she tried to stab me without provocation. I was fuming at her words and the innocent act she was playing. Thankfully Drakari was too strong to be manipulated by a siren song or I'm sure she would have tried that too.

Drakari continued frowning at her, not at all moved by her words. "Laneli, I tried to give you a chance to redeem yourself but attacking a student with a knife and trying to capture a mythical creature is the last straw. I don't know what would have happened if Marion didn't show up and spread the mist everywhere."

I titled my head and furrowed by eyebrows in confusion. Marion looked even more confused and started to speak up to ask what he meant by mist but Drakari gave her a pointed look. Suddenly I understood. Drakari was trying to protect Tam by making it seem as if Marion had caused the smoke. Marion was a water myth blessed so mist would be believable. I smiled at his ingenious cover up.

Drakari turned his attention back to Laneli. “For your unacceptable behavior today and for the past two years, I have no choice but to expel you from Myth Blessed Academy. You will be escorted off campus later today once you pack your things.”

Laneli stood by the high back chair with her mouth agape. I was expecting her to argue his decision but instead she looked at me with hatred and flung herself toward me, trying to scratch my face. I jumped from the chair and backpedaled, avoiding the attack and her nails barely missed my skin. Harvey darted forward, wrapping his arms around her to keep her contained. She stared at me with a look that promised revenge before Harvey stepped back into the shadows and transported them away. I let out a breath I didn’t realize I was holding. Marion gripped my arm and I noticed she was as shook as I was by Laneli’s attack.

“Tamara should be safe now,” Drakari said.

I could hear an edge in his voice that was the only indication that he was disturbed by Laneli’s actions. Otherwise he sat back in his chair with his fingers steepled and kept a neutral expression on his face.

My heart was still racing at the events of the past half hour but now I felt as if I could relax a bit. Elliot would be pleased to know that he will not have to worry about Laneli anymore. In fact, the feud might even end completely. Marion and I shuffled out of the office and once the door closed, we let out a deep breath.

"That was insane," Marion commented softly, ending the silence she had fallen into since getting to the office.

I nodded, not feeling like I could speak just yet. Everything was sorted out, but Tam was probably still upset at the fact I had almost blown her cover. I quickly sent her a text letting her know that Drakari covered up the truth and she was safe now. I didn't get a reply. I would have to call her later.

"You hungry?" Marion asked, steering us to the cafeteria.

I glanced at her bags that she still carried. "You should drop those off first and meet me there."

Marion blinked down at the bags as if she forgot they were there. "Right."

Marion made an about face and headed towards our room while I continued to the cafeteria, checking my phone along the way hoping for a reply from Tam. A set of footsteps fell in step beside me as I passed a shadowy part of the hallway. I glanced up, not at all surprised to see Harvey. He was frowning and his hands were stuffed into his pockets, but he stayed quiet.

Knowing what he wanted to ask, I filled him in on the events of the past few hours. His frown deepened at the mention of Laneli trying to stab me then his face morphed into concern when I explained that his girlfriend may be in danger. Without a word Harvey stepped into the nearest shadow and disappeared. Presumably to check up on Tamara.

I heaved out a sigh and walked to my usual table in the cafeteria, wanting to wait for Marion before getting food. A heavy body thumped down into a seat beside me causing the table to shake and startled me from my thoughts.

"Hey there," Elliot said grabbing my hand and holding it in his own.

I was stunned. I stared at our joined hands, feeling heat dance between us. I knew that asking me to the dance was almost the same as asking me out, according to every teen chick flick I had ever seen, but I hadn't expected hand holding yet. The show of soft emotion in public had my cheeks reddening and my heart beating faster.

The memories of earlier came to mind and I glanced up at Elliot, excited to share my news. "Laneli was expelled today."

He kept his face calm, but I could tell the news affected him due to his hand tightening around mine. "Why?"

I explained to him in a low voice about the events of my shopping trip and how it ended in Drakari's office. I glanced around as I spoke making sure no one else was listening. I left out the part about Tamara and her djinn powers, but I still didn't want anyone overhearing our conversation. When I finished, he sat back, releasing my hand and crossed his arms over his chest. I tried not to feel cold or saddened by the absence of his heat and contact.

The barely contained fury behind his next words startled me. "She tried to stab you?" Black scales erupted over his arms and parts of his face.

I understood now why he let go of my hand. In this state, he would probably crush my bones or burn them to a crisp. I wasn't worried which surprised me since I had gone up against him before and it had terrified me. He would never hurt me though. I laid a hand on his arm wanting him to calm down and be happy that she was gone. He glanced down at my touch with fondness, but the heat still blazed under his skin.

"Sirens be crazy," I joked, hoping to make him smile and relieve the tension in the air.

It worked. Elliot slung an arm over my shoulders and pulled me in close. He leaned down and whispered in my ear, sending chills down my neck. "You're siren blessed too," he chuckled.

I raised my chin resolutely. "I stand by what I said."

I jumped at the deep laugh that burst from him. I had never heard him laugh like that and it made my own grin break out on my face. Elliot's laugh was officially the best sound ever.

The doors of the cafeteria opened, and Marion walked through, spotting us immediately. Elliot noticed her approach and leaned toward my ear again. "Laneli will pay for trying to hurt you."

Marion's arrival stopped any protest I was going to make and left his ominous promise hanging in the air.

Chapter 15

Oh No They Djinn Not

I checked my phone for the millionth time in two weeks. Ever since the alley incident with Laneli, Tamara had only messaged me once and it was a reply to my first message about her identity being safe in which she replied 'ok.' To my annoyance, my constant harassing of Harvey didn't reveal any of Tam's emotions or opinions. The dance was in two days and I had no idea if Tam was going to prepare with Marion and I or avoid us the entire night.

Panda bumped her head against the back of my knee drawing my attention away from my phone. I put my phone down on the desk in front of me and crouched down to pet her behind her ears. Panda bleated in pleasure and pushed against my hand for more. Energy jolted up my arm and the fire and water within my chest stirred. Over the past week, Panda's energy ran through me, helping me balance my inner elements and strengthen my control. It was a heady feeling that left me wanting more but I was warned by Elliot and Marion that taking too much energy from my familiar could leave us both weak.

A buzz from the desk had me springing up and scrambling for my phone. I expected to see a purple flower on the caller ID indicating a call from Tamara but a picture of a cartoon sun with a smiley face greeted me instead.

"Hello?" I answered, trying not to feel disappointed.

"Serena, I think something is wrong," Rae spoke urgently through the phone.

Her tone made me tense and my breathing came fast. "What happened? Are you ok?"

Rae choked on a sob and my heart clenched for my friend. I began pacing, feeling impatient for her answer and helpless that I couldn't be there with her. I imagined her freckled face flushed as tears ran free. Whatever it was, it was serious but what could cause Rae to be so upset?

"It's Tam, I think something happened to her," She finally answered.

I froze. I couldn't speak for fear that if I did then Rae's words would be true. They couldn't be true. What could possibly happen to a powerful djinn? Images of purple smoke in an alley and Laneli popped into my head. Did Tam run away thinking she wasn't safe around us anymore? No, that couldn't be it. Rae would have mentioned a note left behind or said that Tam's whole family was moving. Rae sounded scared and worried.

"Why do you say that?" I asked slowly, afraid of the answer.

Rae sniffled before answering. "Well, I just talked to her last night and we had plans to go to Tang's tonight. When I went to pick her up her parents informed me that she was out with a friend."

I was getting impatient. I continued pacing and wished Rae would get to the part about what was wrong with Tam.

Rae continued, oblivious to my impatience. "I immediately thought of Harvey, so I called him, but he had no idea where she was either. We searched for her for hours and just now discovered her phone laying on her bed."

"Is Harvey there with you now?" I asked, imagining the two of them standing in Tam's room staring down at the abandoned phone.

"Yes," Rae replied.

Harvey must have transported them to the room. I understood now why Rae called. If Tam wasn't with Rae or Harvey, and she didn't take her phone then something was wrong. That djinn loved her phone and I hated to say it but Rae, Harvey and I were her only friends. There was no way she would be out with someone else without one of us knowing about it. Also, did I mention that Tam loved her phone?

It could all be nothing but worry gnawed at me. I needed to be there with them to help search. I grabbed my purse and shoved my keys inside. Now I just needed to find a way there.

"Tell Harvey-" My words were cut off by a cloud of purple smoke.

Relief washed through me at the sight of the smoke and I waited to see the familiar black curls of my friend. Tamara appeared in front of me and I broke out into a relieved grin. I was about to tell Rae the good news but something in Tam's expression stopped me. Her demeanor was off, and she was standing like a silent statue, yet her eyes pleaded with me. My friend was there in front of me but also missing.

"Tam? Are you ok? Rae and Harvey have been looking for you," I said slowly while putting the phone on speaker. Tam was giving off a dangerous vibe and I wanted Rae to hear everything in case her and Harvey needed to assist me right away.

Tam took a step forward and reached out her hand toward me. Her hand shook and pain flashed in her eyes. She was struggling but I couldn't tell with what.

I went to take a step toward her, but Panda jumped in front of my legs and screamed at me in that eerie human-like way. Startled, I jumped back, and Panda butted her head against my shins wanting me to step back further. I glanced from Panda to Tam trying to figure out why my familiar wanted me to stay away.

"Tamara, what is going on? You're scaring me," I said with a raised voice so Rae could hear me clearly.

Tam took another step forward and reached out to grab me. On instinct, I avoided her grip and took a couple more steps away. I wasn't going to be a fool and ignore my familiar's warnings. Plus, Tam was looking at me in a way that sent chills down my spine. The sound of banging on my bedroom door distracted Tam for a moment.

"Serena! Tam! Let us in!" Rae's voice sounded through the door.

Harvey must have transported them to the dorm. I looked around my room and found no shadows big enough for a person to walk through. That was why they didn't appear in the room. Stupid lights. The hallway must hold the closest shadow big enough for two people. I raced toward the door, hoping to slide past Tam while she was distracted and let Harvey and Rae inside. Maybe they could snap Tam out of whatever trance she seemed to be in.

With lightning quick movements, Tam whipped around and grabbed my arm in a viselike grip. Her eyes pooled with tears as she held me firmly.

"Tam, let go!" I was going to have bruises in the shape of a hand if she didn't let go of me soon.

Her body was shaking but her grip held strong. Fire danced in my belly wanting to be released but I couldn't in good conscience barbeque my friend. I thought about using my siren song but even if I was ok with that it wouldn't work because she was a mythological being. Panda bleated loudly and attempted to head butt Tam, but she was unfazed by the baby goat's efforts.

The door burst open with a loud bang and Harvey stood there with shadows gathering along his ankles. Rae stood behind him with a tear streaked face and frightened eyes. I couldn't tell if she was frightened from transporting for the first time or seeing her friend death gripping her other friend.

The last thing I saw was Harvey lunging forward to grab Tam before a cloud of purple smoke enveloped me and I was transported away.

My feet hit something hard a moment later and the smoke disappeared to reveal the mysterious destination, but I still couldn't see anything. I blinked rapidly to adjust my eyes and a soft light outlined a cement room with dancing blue designs on the walls. The dancing designs reminded me of water reflecting onto a wall from an aquarium.

"Hello?" I called out.

Tamara was nowhere to be seen and there were no sounds in the room except for my deep, shaky breaths. My ears were starting to hurt from the intense silence. I hated the dark. Not as much as water, but dark was almost up there with my other irrational fears.

Well, I was not going to just stand there and wait for someone to appear. I took slow steps, to avoid running into obstacles, in the direction of the soft light hoping that the source would give me answers. When I got closer, the sounds of dripping water came from around the corner. I waited a moment and heard no voices, so I ventured around the corner and saw a large tank of water with some light shining through. I knew the dancing designs on the walls looked like those from an aquarium, but unlike the usual aquariums this tank was empty of life.

The sight of a metal door off to the side of the tank filled me with hope and I ran for it. I yanked at the doorknob, but the door didn't budge. Letting out a cry of frustration and despair, I pulled and pulled but the door still did not move. I didn't realize I was crying until strands of hair stuck to my face and my nose started running from the emotions flooding out. I banged on the door with all my might until my energy was spent. I slid along the door to the ground and closed my eyes, trying to reign in the tears and terror. I leaned forward to hug my knees and rested my head on my arms. Eventually I fell asleep, which I didn't think was possible in that situation. I didn't know how long I was out until I heard a noise from the other side.

The door unlocking from the other side had me bolting up and facing the newcomer in a defensive stance. I urged my chimera blessed fire energy to build within my belly. Embarrassingly, my belly growled in hunger, but I ignored it and built up the fire. I would blast whoever was on the other side and make a run for it. The metal door creaked open and light burst into the dim room making me squint until my eyes adjusted. The fire died down when I saw who was on the other side.

"Nurse Lydia?" I asked incredulously.

Her smile turned into disgust. "Don't call me that," she scolded disdainfully.

I jumped back from her tone and without thinking I breathed fire at her. The flames traveling up my throat and out of my mouth didn't feel weird anymore. In this moment it felt right and all I wanted to do was escape.

Nurse Lydia screeched and swatted at her smoking shirt. I took the opportunity to run by her and down the hall. I heard screeches and moans from nearby rooms, but I didn't stop to discover the sources. That place was going to give me nightmares later.

Purple smoke appeared in front of me and relief swept through me. Tamara would get me out of there. Tamara appeared and held out her hands toward me. I stopped in my tracks when I saw the same blank look as before and choked on a sob.

This was not my friend.

Tam jumped forward and wrapped one hand around my mouth and one over my upper arm. She cut off any way for me to use my gifts or escape. I could probably still breathe fire but that meant burning the hand off my best friend and even though she wasn't herself at the moment, I was not going to hurt her.

An annoying laughter sounded behind us and Tam strong-armed me into turning around to face it. I groaned under Tam's hand. I should have known Laneli would have some part in this whole messed up situation.

Laneli walked up to us until she was inches from my face. She sneered at me and glanced at Tam with a gleam in her eye. "You know, it took me a while to figure out what happened that day."

I wanted to spit fire at her or sing to her and make her walk for miles until she was on the other side of the world, but Tam's hand prevented me from doing it.

"Once I figured out your little friend here was a djinn, I just needed to track her down and chant the ancient words," Laneli explained with a smug smile.

My eyes widened in horror. Oh, not they did not! My Tamara was a djinn slave now? Tam once told me the difference between djinns and genies was that djinns had to grant unlimited requests and orders if they were enslaved. My heart broke for her. She had spent eighteen years hiding from the world so this would not happen. Guilt weighed me down because Tam would not be there if I didn't call her to the alley that day.

Lydia walked up behind her daughter and shouldered her out of the way, so she was the one facing me. "Actually, it was me who tracked her down and spoke the words. Either way, she is ours now."

Laneli scowled at her mother but didn't say anything. Lydia crooked her finger at us and walked away, leaving Tam to bring me along. We headed back to the concrete room I had appeared in and I tried to go limp or dig in my feet to make it harder to bring me along, but Tam was magically strong. Within a minute I was back in the dim room with dancing water designs reflecting on the walls from the large tank.

Tam released my mouth and I wasted no time in using it. "Why am I here?" I asked, thoroughly confused. "How long have I been here?"

Lydia's eyes lit up in excitement and she faced the tank. "Only a few hours. I run an operation here that tests mythological beings and their capabilities and eventually I convince them to bless my people." Lydia pinched Laneli's cheek. "That's how my little siren got her blessing."

My mouth fell open in shock. Laneli's blessing was forced. How could Lydia even 'convince' a myth to bless someone? Memories of the attempted naiad abduction at Myth Blessed Academy came to mind.

"Are you a Hunter?" I tried to step away from the dangerous woman, but Tam held me in place.

Lydia scowled. "I am nothing like those vile humans. I collect myths and use them like we should have been doing all these years. What is the point in leaving it to chance when I could control who gets blessed and by which myth?" Lydia shrugged as if it all made sense and she wasn't a crazy lady.

Lydia had all the perfect opportunities to get information about myth being locations. She conducted questionnaires of students, although I'm starting to think she only questioned me, and she had access to student files. I needed to get out of there and warn Drakari. She could build an army of myth blessed people if she hadn't already.

I shook my head, still confused. "I'm not a myth though, so why am I here?" And where was here?

Lydia and Laneli gave me a wicked grin. I was not going to like what they said.

"Take her up there and chain her feet," Laneli ordered Tamara.

Tamara stiffened but complied. She dragged me over to the tank as I kicked out and shouted at her to let go. My heart raced, and my body tingled with dread. Tamara hauled me up a set of stairs next to the tank and stood me up on a metal platform above the water.

"We need to study you and your capabilities, ducky," Lydia called up to me as Tam shackled my ankles with a heavy chain. "You are the only recorded student to be blessed by two myths. If I can figure out how that happened and what it does to you then I can start blessing my people with more than one myth," She exclaimed, excited by the possibilities.

"I'm thinking dragon next for me, mom," Laneli suggested as she smirked at me.

My thoughts went to Elliot. He was the only known dragon blessed and a powerful one at that. If Laneli became dragon blessed on top of her siren one, then she would be unstoppable. Did they have a dragon in house? That seemed impossible, but so did having tons of myths locked up and getting them to bless people on command.

Tam finished chaining me and walked away, leaving me on the platform suspended over calm water.

Lydia produced a clipboard from behind her back and took out a pen that laid behind her ear. "Test one, underwater tolerance."

I heard a click, the platform gave way underneath me, and then I was tumbling into the water. I sucked in a lungful of air before I was submerged but it would not last. The chains dragged me down and soon I was sitting at the bottom of the tank staring out at three blurry figures. My chest constricted and a weight seemed to press me from the inside. My hands shook with fright and panic. I struggled to swim upward toward air, but the chains were too heavy. My hope for survival diminished by the second. My lungs burned until I couldn't hold it any longer. My mouth opened to suck in air, but water flooded in instead.

This was it. I was going to die.

Chapter 16

Escaping the Zoo

I expected to die right away but I was still waiting. I floated there, my hair waving around in the water, and waited. A face appeared against the glass showcasing an annoying amount of makeup. I gasped at her sudden appearance then gasped again when I realized that I just sucked in water but could still breathe.

I could breathe underwater!

Marion would be so happy to hear about this new development. That is, if she ever got to hear about it.

Lydia smiled at me with satisfaction and marked something on her clipboard. I may not have drowned but there were more ways Lydia and her evil siren blessed offspring could kill me. I took in another breath of water and couldn't stop the smile when my lungs filled with air instead.

My chest tightened suddenly, even though I could still breathe, my hands shook with panic reminding me that my chimera side didn't like the water. I struggled to swim up again, but the chains pulled me down.

How long were they going to keep me in the tank?

My answer came an hour later when purple smoke settled around me and I was transported back in front of Lydia. The chain clanged loudly against the cement floor and water fell off me in streams. The chill hit me hard and I wrapped my arms around myself to contain the escaping warmth.

Even though that led to the discovery of being able to breathe underwater, I was done with the experiments. I had two powerful gifts and it was time I used one of them.

The water energy was heightened since I had just been surrounded by it. I opened my mouth to sing, not caring at the moment if my siren ability took away their will. They took mine away by submerging me in the water and they took Tam's away when they enslaved her.

One beautiful note escaped before Tam's hand slapped over my mouth and silenced me. I slumped in defeat. There was no way to escape without burning my friend's hand off. Lydia was going to pay for using my best friend against me.

"That was a successful test," Lydia exclaimed. "Now let's go test fire."

Laneli chuckled nearby which reminded me of Disney villains and their evil laughs. Lydia bent down and unlocked my chains. I was tempted to kick her in the face but that would probably backfire somehow, so I refrained. Lydia opened the door and led us down the same hall we came from earlier. Water left a path behind me as I trudged down the hall and my sneakers squeaked loudly in the emptiness.

Moans and scrapes against metal sounded as we passed by closed doors further down the hall. Eventually the locked doors turned into cages and I could see all sorts of mythological beings trapped behind bars. Each cage had a name plate on the outside explaining the name and origin of the beings. It was as if we were in a zoo. I started with horror when I realized I was one of the zoo animals.

A satyr peered out at me through the bars of one cage and his goat legs reminded me of Panda causing a pang of loneliness to pierce my heart. As we continued, I saw strange and gross looking mythological beings that I had never heard of before such as a frightening worm from Mongolia called a Mongolian death worm and a grotesque animal called a bunyip from Australia. Then there were those that I did recognize from stories or myth history class such as a gargoyle, a kelpie, and an Egyptian ammit.

I stumbled to a stop when I locked eyes with a siren floating in a tank of water. Her blonde hair drifted around her like a halo and her piercing blue eyes seemed to draw me closer. I could imagine how enchanting her songs must be, but I knew from experience that those songs could be dangerous. I wondered if that was the siren that blessed Laneli.

Tamara propelled me forward again, breaking my eye contact with the siren. Soon, we came up to another door at the end of the hall and Lydia keyed in a code before leading us in. A bed of coals laid in the middle of the floor, spanning five feet by five feet. Lydia flipped a switch nearby and fire sprang up from the coals high into the air. I jumped back as a blast of heat hit my face. I shrunk away from the flames wanting to be far away from whatever test was next. The same aching in my chest that I had in the water returned with a vengeance and my hands shook in fear. This time it was my siren side that recoiled.

"We have a room for each of the elements to test beings and blessed humans," Lydia explained.

I forced my wide eyes to focus on Lydia instead of the giant fire in the room. "Why are you torturing those myths?" I finally asked.

Lydia frowned. "I am a scientist. I am doing what the government should have done years ago." Lydia looked at Tam over my shoulder. "Now, throw her into the fire."

I knew the fire wouldn't hurt me, but I still struggled and pleaded with them. My efforts were useless because Tam was forced to follow orders and Lydia and Laneli didn't care about their test subject's feelings. Flames engulfed me and heat filled every pore. Sweat immediately beaded on my skin and the flames licked at my clothes. Just like the water, I was able to breathe normally, and the fire didn't hurt. It felt like warm feathers tickling my skin.

Even though it didn't hurt, I did not want to stick around to find out how long I would be kept there or how many more tests I would be subjected to. Since I was not chained down that time, and the bed of coals had open sides, I was able to stand and jump out of the fire. I knew I would not have long to act so I called on my heightened fire energy and let loose the pressure building in my belly. Fire roared out of my mouth and shrieks came from the direction of Lydia and Laneli. I was sickeningly hoping they got turned to ash.

I used the distraction to race to the door and flung it open. I knew as soon as Lydia was able to speak, Tam would be on my tail in less than a second. Which meant escape was impossible.

Changing my plan, I ran to each cage and melted the locks with my fire breath. Once the locks were gone the mythological beings burst from their cages, causing chaos. I had to flatten myself against walls to avoid hooves and talons, but I managed to release over ten beings.

Purple smoke appeared in front of me and I knew my time was up. Tamara appeared with a group of tall, beefy men behind her. They reminded me of the men that tried to kidnap the naiad at the Academy. I mentally facepalmed. I should have figured it out sooner. Those men weren't traditional Hunters, they were Lydia's collection Hunters. That is why the men at the lake were abducting not killing. I wondered if the SMP knew about the two Hunter factions.

Tam stepped aside and two men rushed over to me and tied me up with rough rope. A nasty smelling cloth was placed over my mouth which snagged a few hairs as it was tied behind my head. A tsking sound made its way over to me and Lydia appeared with hairs astray and charred clothes but sadly no burns. I really hoped my fire breath would have taken her out of commission. I noticed Laneli was not there so maybe I accomplished something.

"Take her back to the water room," Lydia ordered the men holding me as she glared daggers that promised revenge.

I was roughly led down the hall by two Hunters while the others tried to catch and contain the escaped myths. This whole situation was messed up. These myths did not deserve to be locked up and experimented on. Tamara did not deserve to be a djinn slave to a crazy Hunter scientist. The only thing that seemed fair was the fact that I was here with all of them. If I didn't make that mistake in calling Tam to the alley, then Laneli wouldn't have figured out my best friend was a djinn. I deserved whatever torture they gave me.

Despite my gloomy thoughts, I felt anger simmering deep within my belly. I would release all those myths and my best friend if it was the last thing I did. I tried spitting out the foul-tasting cloth, but it only caused my tongue to taste more of it. I would have to wait to fight back once the cloth was removed and the guards were not securely holding me.

Movement from my left drew my attention. We already passed the cages so all I saw were locked doors. I could have sworn I saw something move in the shadows though, but as I peered into the darkness surrounding each door there was no other movement. I shook my head and faced forward again trying to figure out a plan to get out of there.

We reached the water room a moment later and one of the guards tightened his grip on my arms while the other keyed in a code to let us in. The guard holding me roughly shoved me forward into the room while keeping his hold on me. I had only been there for a few hours, but the water room was already familiar. The tank cast watery light onto the walls and the room echoed with the sound of dripping.

I was startled by a chair being slammed in front of me. The Hunter holding me forced me to sit while the other tied me to the chair. Once I was secure the Hunters moved to stand by the door, leaving me to stare at the slightly lighted tank of water.

It was interesting how this whole new life of mine started with water. A beautiful song and a swim caused me to become blessed for apparently the second time. Then, suddenly, I was at Myth Blessed Academy with one crazy thing happening after another. All because of water.

Movement from the side of the tank, near the shadows, caught my attention. This time I was one hundred percent sure there was something there. My eyes couldn't focus enough to see what it was, but I was almost certain it was the same thing I glimpsed in the hallway. I glanced behind me at the two Hunters to see if they saw anything, but they stared straight ahead like good little soldiers. A moment later, shapes appeared in the shadows and my heart almost burst with happiness.

Elliot and Harvey stood camouflaged in the shadows near the tank. Harvey must have grabbed onto Tam in time when she transported me away then went to get back up when he figured out where we landed. I saw Elliot's mouth move but I was not very good at reading lips. I frowned and tilted my head a little in confusion.

He mouthed the words again, this time with hand signals, "Are you ok?"

Since I couldn't say anything back or use hand signals, I was stuck with using my facial expressions. I deepened my frown and glared at him, hoping he could read the *what do you think* sarcasm I was throwing at him.

Elliot held up one finger telling me to wait a minute and turned to say something to Harvey. Wait for what I had no idea. Plus, I really didn't have a choice. I pulled against the ropes that held me to the chair but there was no give. I wished I could control fire with my hands like a normal fire myth blessed. I squinted, trying to see them better, but I could only make out their shapes. I would be surprised if the Hunters saw them, since they were on the other side of the room, but I still felt fearful for my friends.

Elliot turned back to me and I could see something like determination in his face, but the shadows made it unclear. Elliot took one step forward and my eyes widened in panic. He was going to step out from the shadows. I knew he could handle the two guards, but I was still worried. Before Elliot could step all the way out and announce his presence, the door to the water room opened and Lydia, followed by her djinn slave, entered the room. I shook my head at Elliot hoping he knew that I was telling him to stay back. Elliot and Harvey could handle a couple of beefy Hunter dudes, but they were no match for a djinn.

"That was quite a ruckus you caused back there," Lydia scolded, oblivious to the two powerful myth blessed in the corner. She appeared in my line of sight and bent down toward me, smiling. "We got all the myths locked back up, but it was a bold move on your part to try."

I rolled my eyes since it was the only thing I could do. I tried to put up a brave front but, on the inside, I was terrified of what her punishment would be.

"Before we continue, someone would like to say something." Lydia crooked a finger at someone over my shoulder.

I craned my neck to see who it was, and my stomach dropped. I knew it was too good to be true that she was gone. Laneli stepped up beside her mother and glared at me. If it wasn't for the fact that I was tied up and gagged, I would have laughed until my stomach hurt at Laneli's missing eyebrows and singed clothes and hair. Even then, I couldn't help the mirth gleaming in my eyes and the shakes in my shoulders as I tried to hold back the laughter.

My humor immediately died when pain suddenly radiated out from my jaw through my face to the top of my head. I shook my head to focus and saw Laneli standing over me with a clenched fist.

Her fist flew toward my face again and all I could do was close my eyes and brace for impact. The second punch knocked my head back and blackness threatened to take over. When I opened my eyes, I glanced behind Laneli and saw Harvey's shape restraining Elliot's shadowed shape. I shook my head at them to tell them to stay put then regretted the movement as sharp pains tore through my skull.

“Let me do it.” Laneli held out her hand to her mother. “I want to see her suffer,” Laneli hissed.

She reminded me of a snake with that hissing and the venom she so obviously held against me. If I didn’t know any better, she could have been a lamia myth blessed. I blinked a few times, trying to focus on the two women.

Lydia smiled at her daughter and handed over a pink pill. I narrowed my eyes at them, instantly suspicious of that pill. It looked innocent enough but Laneli was the one holding it which automatically meant something was wrong, and she had just said she wanted to cause me suffering. I did not want any part of that. Laneli smiled at me in a way that I expected fangs to drop down out of her snake mouth. Laneli must have hit me hard for me to have so many snake analogies however, they were accurate.

“If you sing or spew your filthy fire at me, your little friend here will snap your neck,” Laneli threatened as she gestured to Tam.

I just sat silent and glared at her. I did not know if Laneli’s threat was true, especially since Lydia needed me for more experiments, but I figured I should take it to heart. No need for snapped necks today.

Laneli yanked at the knot of the gag behind me and pulled the cloth away, taking a few of my hairs with it. Tears stung my eyes at the sharp pain from having hair roughly pulled out, but I figured it was better than a snapped neck. Laneli leaned over and squeezed my cheeks, forcing me to open my mouth. Her other hand, holding the pill, drew nearer and my heart started to race. I assumed the pill wouldn't kill me, but in my experience, experience being from movies, that pill would not be good to have in my system. I tried to move my head away from her hands, but her grip was strong.

"Stop struggling," Laneli gritted out as she attempted to hold my head in place. When I didn't listen, she slapped me, causing stars to dot my vision.

I hissed at her and twisted my head sharply, so her hand was near my mouth. Without thinking, I bit down as hard as I could, and liquid filled my mouth. I thought her blood would taste like copper, but it tasted sweet.

Laneli screeched, dropped the pill and stumbled back, cradling her hand. "Kill her," Laneli screamed at Tam.

My eyes darted to my friend and I saw a small smirk on her lips. Relief washed through me at that smile. My friend was not completely gone. Tam ignored the request making me wonder who really had control over the djinn. Lydia tsked at her daughter then strode over to the pill and picked it up.

"You shouldn't have done-" Lydia started but was cut off by Laneli gasping in pain.

We looked over in time to watch Laneli crumple to the floor and writhe in pain. "Make it stop, it burns," Laneli cried out.

Lydia rushed over and knelt next to her. I couldn't see Laneli very well since Lydia blocked her, but I caught a glimpse of a swollen hand with two puncture wounds.

"Go get bandages and my medical kit," Lydia yelled at the guards near the door. "Find an antivenom serum."

I didn't turn to see them leave but I heard the door close behind them. I was still tied to the chair and could only look on in horror as Laneli screamed in pain and writhed on the floor. How could that happen? There were no snakes in the room, and Laneli was completely fine a second ago.

Lydia turned to me with rage in her eyes and a little bit of fear. She stood up and walked slowly to me with clenched fists and her skin turned red with anger and worry. "What kind Chimera crap did you do?"

Chimera? She was accusing me of poisoning her daughter with venom, but she had to be wrong. I didn't have a venomous bite.

Then again, a chimera was part lion, goat, and snake. I had been thinking of snakes wherever Laneli was concerned, so maybe…

"Tell me the antidote, you Chimera monster!" Lydia screamed at me and shook my shoulders. Her nails dug into my skin through my clothing making me wince.

"I-I don't know," I told her honestly.

I glanced at Laneli and remembered the sweet taste when I bit into her hand. Maybe that was the venom I tasted rather than blood. Would I never not have a surprising new gift? My stomach clenched with guilt over Laneli's pain, but I had just wished her dead less than an hour before.

Maybe I was a monster after all.

"Djinn," Laneli summoned, "make her pay for this."

Tamara moved forward though she seemed to struggle against it. Purple smoke started to surround her hands and I could only imagine what would follow. She looked sorrowful but her actions continued to follow the order.

Lydia suddenly screamed in pain and Tamara froze as if her orders were halted. Lydia began to look ashen and the color leeched from her skin. I looked on horrified and unable to do anything as she crumpled to the floor in front of me. Harvey, cloaked in shadows, stood behind her with a glowing pink and blue orb in his hand.

I stared at him with wide eyes and mouth agape then at the glowing colorful orb.

Harvey shrugged. "Nalusa Chito," he said then shoved the orb into his mouth. If I didn't see it with my own eyes, I would not have believed her just did that. He actually ate the glowing orb he took from Lydia's body.

I gagged and looked away from the frightening and sickening sight.

"Soul eater," I whispered once I got my stomach under control. I slowly looked back at him, completely grossed out by his scary gift. No wonder Drakari continued to bring him along on missions. Despite not having a familiar, he was one powerful myth blessed.

Harvey had the decency to look embarrassed but immediately replaced it with relief when he saw Tamara. My friend had unfrozen and now looked clear headed. Killing her master must have released her bond. Harvey and Tam embraced, and I choked on a sob. We had her back and she was free now.

The doors burst open and five Hunters stormed through. They looked from us to the collapsed body of their boss and dove to attack Harvey who stood close to the door. Before they could touch Tam or Harvey, Elliot roared, and a column of fire raced toward the Hunters. Elliot's skin was covered in black scales and his fingers seemed to be longer and sharper, almost like talons. Elliot picked up one of the men and tossed him at a wall as if his weight was that of a feather. Then he slashed out at two more, causing large gashes to appear on their chests. The other two Hunters stared at Elliot then their comrades and ran frightened from the room. I would be frightened too if I faced a dragon blessed in combat.

Elliot ran to me and quickly untied me. As soon as those ropes were gone, I was crushed against a solid chest and wrapped with dragon scaled arms. I held back my wince as my bruised cheek was smooshed against him and inhaled his campfire scent.

"That was the most frightening thing I ever had to witness," Elliot breathed into my ear and held me closer.

"The whole Lydia and Laneli thing or Harvey's new appetite?" I joked, trying to lighten the mood.

He leaned back and smiled. "Ya know? You are one tough myth blessed." His smile almost made me cry because I never thought I would see it again, yet here it was. He rubbed my cheek with the pad of his thumb and his eyes darkened fiercely. His statement about my toughness and the anger simmering in his eyes reminded me of Laneli and how my toughness was just a defense mechanism.

I glanced over at her and saw that she had become still. My venom had moved through her system too quickly. I couldn't hold it back any longer. I broke down and cried against Elliot's chest. My friend had been a slave to a crazy scientist, I had been kidnapped and tortured, and innocent myths were held captive in a weird zoo-like facility, yet it was Laneli's death that hit me the hardest. This whole time I was terrified of my siren side, but it was my chimera side that caused the most damage.

Chapter 17

Blessing or a Curse

Panda butted her little goat head against my shin, wanting my attention. I had been spacing out for the last couple of days, my mind replaying all the events from the facility, and I hadn't been giving her the attention she needed.

We had called Dominic Drakari and the SMP once we dealt with the Hunter guards that night. I was numb after my crying session and ended up singing to anyone who came nearby, not caring about their free will at the time. I was already a monster so what was one more thing on my list. I effectively created an army of enchanted Hunters who I put to work freeing the caged myths. It was ironic that the Hunters who captured those creatures were the ones to set them free. SMP showed up shortly after and took our statements and helped get the myths back to their proper regions.

Knocking on my door alerted me just before someone opened it and danced inside. Seeing Marion brought me back to the present and I picked up Panda to stroke her fur. Marion looked happy and excited in her aqua ball gown. Her hair glittered in the light and her dress reminded me of the lake behind our dorms. For once her hair was down and laid curled against her back. She stopped dancing when she saw me at my desk and a look of pity crossed her face before she masked it with a smile.

"Why aren't you ready yet," she scolded me and glanced at my dress laying on the bed.

It was a beautiful and elegant gold dress with blue shimmers in it. The dress reminded me of my dual myths and that was probably what Tamara was going for when she magicked it into existence yesterday. She said she held no hard feelings against me and that the whole thing was not my fault, but I couldn't bring myself to believe her. She had become a slave because I drew attention to her.

As if summoned by my thoughts, purple smoke filled the room and a djinn in a short frilly purple dress appeared in our room. Tamara rested her hands on her hips and glared at me.

"Why are you not dressed yet?" Tamara asked incredulously.

"That's what I asked too," Marion shouted and stood next to Tam, mimicking her hands-on-hips pose.

I grimaced at the dress on my bed. It had only been two days since I killed Laneli and I felt like I would be sick anytime I thought of her screams or swollen hand. I was about to let them down and say I wasn't going but cold liquid suddenly engulfed my head. It poured over my hair and down my face causing my clothes to become soaked. I shrieked and stood up, dumping Panda on the floor as I tried to escape more water.

"What was that?" I spluttered in outrage.

"Now you have to change and get your head in the game," Marion chuckled.

Marion and Tamara dropped to the floor in fits of laughter, clenching their stomachs at my drowned rat appearance. I couldn't help the smile that came to my own lips and soon we were all laughing and rolling on the floor. It felt nice to laugh again and feel loved by my friends.

Fine, I would put on the stupid dress and go to the stupid dance. I stood up and held my arms open waiting for them to catch on. When they didn't, I sighed and titled my chin up in fake haughtiness.

"It is only fit that you clean me up since you two are the ones to make me look like this," I squeezed my lips shut, fighting the grin that wanted to break free.

The girls stared at me then stated laughing again. I put my hands on my hips and looked in the mirror. The grin finally broke through at seeing my drenched appearance trying to act tough.

"Alright, alright, but seriously, can you help me?" I held my arms out again and looked to Tam, our resident magical djinn.

She rolled her eyes but stood up and waved her hands at me, purple smoke following her command. As usual the smoke did not smell or feel odd as it surrounded me and as usual, something amazing happened in its wake.

I turned to the mirror when the smoke cleared and gasped at my reflection. I was completely dry and dressed in my ankle length golden dress that shimmered blue as I turned. My hair was done up in curls and pulled back so only a couple ringlets fell around my face. Tamara did a great job.

A knock on the door sent flutters through my chest. My palms became sweaty and my heart began to race in response to who must be on the other side. Tamara opened our door and jumped into the arms of a well-dressed Nalusa Chito blessed. Behind Harvey stood Devon with a handkerchief in his breast pocket that matched the color of Marion's dress and a smile that had love written all over it.

Finally, Devon and Harvey moved aside, and my breath caught. Elliot still sported his spiky black hair but seeing him in a tuxedo made it hard to breathe. He smirked as if he knew how he affected me and walked over until he was standing only inches away. I had never seen someone more gorgeous than Elliot Maganot in that moment.

“You are beautiful, Serena,” Elliot complimented and produced a lily corsage from behind his back.

I smiled at the flower and held out my wrist. Elliot carefully took the flower from the container it was stored in and wrapped it around my wrist with a silk ribbon. I beamed at him and felt my cheeks heat at the formality of his behavior.

“Ready to go?” Harvey asked the group.

I continued staring into Elliot’s copper eyes and nodded. Fire seemed to dance within his irises as he smiled down at me and took my hand to lead me from the room.

Baaa

I turned to Panda and pointed to my bed. “Panda, stay. We don’t need you head butting anyone tonight.”

Panda responded by headbutting the back of my leg and bleating. I chuckled and picked her up. “I will be fine.”

My chest clenched in fear that maybe I wouldn’t be fine, but my familiar didn’t need to know that. It would only worry her. I rested the baby goat on my bed and walked from the room with Elliot in tow.

The dance was in the cafeteria, yet I almost didn’t recognize the room. All the tables had been pushed to the side and lights and streamers hung from the ceiling. Music was already playing when we arrived, and bodies moved in rhythm out on the dance floor. Marion and

Devon joined the dancing group and Tam and Harvey went to grab a table.

I glanced up at Elliot to see what he wanted to do and the way he looked at me made me gasp. His eyes were intense but in a protective and I-want-you way. His hands glided across my arms down to my hands, leaving trails of heat in their wake. He leaned forward a fraction of an inch, silently asking me if he could get closer. I held my breath and stood still in case I somehow ruined that perfect moment. Elliot brought his head closer and softly brushed his lips against mine.

I didn't realize I was still frozen and hadn't even closed my eyes to enjoy the kiss until Elliot pulled back and stared into my eyes. I was just shocked that someone as tough and brilliant as Elliot wanted to kiss me. For the first time I could see vulnerability and doubt in his gaze. I did not want him ever to feel that way around me. I grabbed the front of his suit and pulled him to me, crushing our lips together in the most amazing kiss I ever took part in. I had been kissed before, when I was a freshman, but nothing was as moving or searing like this one. It felt like minutes or hours later that we finally broke apart. I was pleased to see he was just as affected as I felt. We were breathing hard and he seemed to stare into my very soul. Elliot leaned forward again and pressed a softer kiss onto my lips leaving my mind foggy and my heart happy.

"Wanna dance?" He asked, smiling at me.

It took me a moment to understand what he said, my mind still focused on the touch of his lips and hands on my arms. He smirked at my silence, somehow knowing that I was too affected to speak. He led me out to the dance floor, a little away from the large group but still nearby enough that it didn't look weird. He led me in a somewhat slow dance even though the music was more upbeat. I felt my cheeks heating but thankfully the room was more on the dark side so Elliot couldn't have noticed.

"So, I've been reading Nurse Lydia's notes," Elliot whispered.

I froze at the mention of Lydia but uncoiled as Elliot's hands rubbed my arms. I cleared my throat so that my voice would come out strong rather than unnecessarily frightened. "What did you find?"

Elliot spun me around before bringing me back close to him. "They were about the myth experiments she did, the people she got blessed, and many were about you."

A shock jolted me at the fact she had notes on me and my whole being needed to know what she found. "And? What did she have about me?"

Elliot shrugged. "Nothing much. Just observations, that meeting she had with you after fall break, and notes from your time in the facility."

I nodded slowly. I figured that meeting after fall break was odd when she didn't talk to anyone else. Elliot must have gotten a hold of her notes from the facility in addition to the ones in her nurse's office because the notes from the facility had been with her when she…when she died.

"You know, even though she didn't discover how you came to have two myths, I think I figured it out," Elliot said thoughtfully.

His announcement startled me. "You did?" I tried not to feel too excited since it was just a guess, but Elliot had been right about my conflicting elements so his was a good a guess as any.

Elliot nodded and looked off to the side before moving us away from the dancing group a little more. "Nurse Lydia had notes on tons of myths and none of them could reproduce the same outcome as you. Yet, there was one myth she never tried." He looked at me expectantly, waiting for me to catch on to his idea.

I knew for a fact she had tried sirens since she had one bless her daughter but out of all the myths in that facility, I did not see an important one. "She didn't try a chimera."

He nodded and beamed at me, pleased that I realized her mistake. "I started reading up on Chimera's and they live in constant unrest, always struggling with harmony in itself since the lion, snake, and goat are not quite symbiotic."

I nodded in understanding. "So, you think since the chimera blessed me, I was able to hold another blessing because it would make me less harmonious inside just like the myth."

Elliot nodded and I sighed. Well, the chimera got what it wanted. Water and fire do not mix well, and my body struggled with itself every time I tried to use my gifts or get near the elements. If Lydia had come to the same conclusion we had, she could have had an army of very powerful myth blessed. The chimera on its own had tons of gifts but pair that with another powerful myth and…I didn't want to think what could have happened. I still hadn't figured out whether being blessed by two myths was a blessing or a curse. I had gone through so much with these powers in just a few months. I was glad that we finally figured out how it was possible, and my heart warmed toward Elliot for going through all that research and helping me.

I rested my head on his shoulder and chuckled. "Ever thought you, Elliot Maganot, would be dancing with a siren blessed?"

His chest rumbled against my ear as he chuckled. "With you, anything is possible."

My heart fluttered at that statement and we continued to slow dance through two more songs.

After a while, Elliot and I joined Tamara and Harvey at the table, clasping each other's hands, unable to separate. Something more was between us now, whether it was from our kiss or shared revelation of my dual myths. Either way, I was both nervous and excited it was happening.

"I wish Rae could have joined us," Tam pouted across from me.

I pictured my poofy, orange headed friend and chuckled. "Me too, she is probably going to get revenge on us somehow for being excluded." Rae was already grumpy at Harvey for not bringing her to the facility to help rescue us, something I was extremely grateful she missed.

"I'm sorry Tamara," I blurted out.

The three of them blinked at me in confusion. Understanding my meaning, Tamara frowned and slapped my hand that rested on the table. "Do not apologize. My captivity was not your fault, it was Laneli's, who I for one am glad you dealt with." Tamara leaned back and crossed her arms in defiance.

A twinge in my heart and burning in my eyes started at the mention of Laneli's death by venomous bite and Tamara's enslavement. I didn't think I could ever get over those events. Tamara was the strongest person I knew, and I was glad she continued to be my friend even after all of that. I on the other hand felt like I would crumble to pieces at any moment. Looking around me I knew I would have the best people around to help keep me sane.

I didn't want any myth or myth blessed to ever go through something like that. I was powerful, and whether my powers were a gift or a curse, I would use them to keep my friends safe. My plans in Hawaii were to graduate, move across the country, and become an analyst or detective. After everything that had happened, my goals have changed. I would graduate and become an agent of the Society for Mythical Protection. A sense of purpose settled in my belly and for once, without Panda, my dual myths were aligned and at peace.

Acknowledgements

I want to thank Victoria Gillette for continuously being supportive and willing to read my books. I always appreciate her feedback. I quite literally wouldn't be here today if it wasn't for her.

I want to thank Phoenix Designs from 99designs for giving me an incredible cover that embodies the character and story exceptionally. Out of all the designers that presented ideas, Phoenix Designs had the best.

Lastly, I would love to acknowledge my readers and all the support they have given me over the past year. You guys have helped me stay in the spirit of writing.

About Author

Katie Dunn grew up in the hot part of Arizona where she graduated NAU and became a teacher. She got a taste of the author life after her first YA contemporary fantasy novel Ancient Elements. Finding out she loved writing just as much as reading, teaching, and traveling, she sat down and wrote the first installment of the YA fantasy adventure Skor Stone trilogy: Pirates from Under and YA contemporary fantasy novel Myth Blessed.

You can check out more about Katie Dunn's books and works in progress at:

Facebook.com/AuthorKatieDunn/

Kdunnauthor.com

Made in United States
Troutdale, OR
06/23/2024